The Fountain

A Novel

Kat Giordano

THIRTY WEST
PUBLISHING HOUSE

The Fountain

ISBN-13: 978-1-7345158-3-1

Cover design by Carolyn Brandt

Product of the U.S.A.

For more titles and inquiries, please visit:

www.thirtywestph.com

Table of Contents

The Fountain

BREAKFAST

Two days after I broke up with Cody, Chris Cornell died. The Soundgarden guy. Cody was a big Soundgarden fan, so when he called me, it wasn't surprising. When I picked up the phone he was in tears and at 7 AM no less—way earlier than I'd ever known him to wake up the whole time we were together. At first, I thought it was just an excuse to get ahold of me, but between sentences, I could hear him taking frantic little breaths like he was seconds away from totally losing it. He didn't even say that he missed me and wanted us to make up. He was just really sad about Chris Cornell.

He kept saying the same things over and over. Speculating about how it might have happened, whether it was a suicide, an accidental overdose, or something else. (Out of all of the guys from that era of music, Chris Cornell was the one he would have least expected to be addicted to something. But that doesn't mean that isn't what happened, right?) He wondered aloud whether Soundgarden would continue making music after this, what would happen to any of the releases they'd already planned, or whether it would be like what happened with Nirvana and the other guys would start some kind of Foo Fighters-esque project to try and pick up where Chris Cornell left off.

After a while I said, "I don't know, it was just announced this morning, you're thinking really far ahead."

He hyperventilated for a second and then said, "We really should have gone to see them a couple of years ago while we still could." He was using that gruff, taking-charge sort of voice he always used when he was trying to prove himself right about something. It always sounded completely manufactured to me, like he'd copped it straight from some kind of "How to Be More Assertive" YouTube video with only 14 views. "But you didn't want to go for some reason."

"I'd just gotten my wisdom teeth out."

"Now I'm never going to see him."

"Well, sorry." I was trying not to sound sour, but I sounded sour. I sighed. "I'm sorry."

He said, "I guess now there's really no point in hoping for another Audioslave album."

"Yeah, I guess not."

I squeezed the phone between my chin and shoulder and grabbed a box of cereal out of the kitchen cabinet. I knew I was being insensitive or whatever, not showing nearly enough interest in this conversation, but I wasn't able to muster any compassion. I'd reached deep down and there just wasn't any there. To me, when celebrities died, it was sad but not overly so. Not in a personal way. I approached it with the same pouty reaction as I did a dead animal on the side of the road. The most I ever said was, "It's really a shame," and I don't even feel like I meant those specific words more than I would have meant any others. It was just a phrase I'd picked up from someone else at some point and had eventually determined was safe to use in this context. Or at least wouldn't provoke the kind of suspicion the other options did.

"It's really a shame," I said.

Cody didn't say anything for a few minutes. His breathing, though, seemed slower; he wasn't doing that about-to-cry thing. He was no longer at red alert, no longer giving me sympathy chest pains from my subconscious efforts to mirror his breathing. I ripped the box of cereal open and tilted it on its side. I no longer cared that he could hear the cereal clinking against the sides of the bowl as I poured.

"...at thing?" Cody said from underneath a mound of Cheerios.

"What?" I paused, jerking the box upwards. A few Cheerios flew forwards, missing the rim of the bowl and landing on the floor in front of my feed. I stepped back, wound up, and kicked them under the fridge.

"Are you still going to that thing?" he repeated.

"The festival thing?"

"Yeah."

"Yeah, I'm going."

"When is it?"

"Tomorrow."

"Did you figure out if you're going to drive there or—?"

"Train." I was talking the way my parents texted, using the absolute minimal amount of characters necessary, employing basic calculus to optimize the quality of conversation while mitigating the exhaustion of typing too many words. Talking to him felt like that right now, like typing with one index finger, like I was holding this conversation in front of me as if I'd never seen such a thing before and pecking at it with just one finger, one sound at a time.

"What time is the train?"

"Seven."

"At night?"

"No."

"Look," Cody said. He stood up inside the bowl like a kid in a ball pit, hands on his hips, trying to look like he Meant Business or something. "I think maybe we both got out of control the other night and I was wondering if you felt the same way." He waded toward me, hoisting his knees halfway up his abdomen. A piece of Cheerio fell out of his sleeve and landed in front of him at waist level. I laughed.

"What?" he said.

"What are you asking me?"

"I'm asking you if you still mean what you said the other day."

"Then yeah."

I pulled a spoon out of the drawer and held it up to the light. There was a little spot on it, most likely just a soapy water stain from drying weirdly or being rinsed improperly but possibly some leftover residue from the last thing it was used for. I decided I didn't care. I plunged the spoon into the bowl, shoving it accidentally-on-purpose right into Cody's shin. He doubled over, clutching his leg, now chest-deep in Cheerios. I pulled the jug of milk out of the fridge and poured until it was empty. The bowl overflowed, and a half cup of milk sloshed onto the floor in front of me, taking Cody and a handful of half-disintegrated wet cereal with it. I hung up the phone and kicked all of it, and him, under the fridge.

The next morning, Sidney picked me up from the train station. It was barely 9:00. She was standing there on the platform wearing a full face of makeup and a jumpsuit. Taken together, these things were a Bad Sign. I knew Sidney well. She didn't get up before 10:00; it just simply wasn't done. For her to be this chipper at this hour—and in full costume nonetheless—could only mean one thing: she'd been up all night, likely due to a combination of Adderall and genuine excitement, likely on the tail of some ridiculous circumstance she would later explain to me over breakfast or lunch.

"You look nice," I said, walking towards her.

"Thanks."

From this distance, it was immediately obvious to me just how right I had been. Her eyes were bloodshot, bigger than usual, the jumpsuit wrinkled. You could see all of the cracks in her façade of alertness, the long night she had painted over. But at that moment, I was worried less for Sidney than I was for myself. None of this was abnormal for her, she always handled things, but between the lack of sleep and the week I'd just had, I wasn't sure how I was going to make it through this day intact.

"It was a little late," I said, gesturing behind me at the train letting out.

"Was it?"

"Yeah. I mean, a little."

"Huh," she said. "Well, whatever."

We climbed the stairs out of the station and headed to the lot where Sidney's car was parked.

"Are you hungry?" she asked. "I already got your coffee, but if you want something more than that, we can stop."

"Yeah, but I can wait. I'm not starving or anything," I lied. Sidney's car was the only one in the lot. She unlocked the doors, and I threw my backpack in the back seat before climbing into the passenger seat beside her.

"Cool. Coffee's there." She gestured toward the paper cup of gas-station coffee situated in the cup holder to my left. I took a sip, letting it scald me on the way down. There's this special thing that happens with coffee when you've delayed it a while but haven't quite hit the withdrawal stage. You can feel the caffeination happening: a wilted plant in your chest being watered. As Sidney started the car, it was like I rumbled to life with it, feeling more human suddenly.

We pulled out of the parking lot, taking with us any evidence that a train had ever stopped there. Taking public transportation in the suburbs felt alienating. The existence of bus and train stations in places like this felt like more of a technicality than something ever intended for use. It was there to fulfill some arbitrary, maybe antiquated, definition of a Town, a theoretical but not necessarily viable option for a population that largely had their cars or enough money for a more pleasant way to travel. This was perhaps especially true for Sidney's hometown, which, as we chugged down Main Street, looked its usual flavor of deserted. I always got the sense that Sidney's festival was the most action this place saw all year, which was especially telling given that it was barely a festival at all.

I stared out the passenger-side window. "I always forget there are, like, actual trees here," I said.

"There are trees back home."

"You know what I mean, though. Like, natural trees."

"Natural trees," Sidney repeated.

"Yeah, like, some guy didn't plant these here a few years ago. 'Oh, I should cut out a little square of the sidewalk.'" We were both laughing a little. "You know what I mean."

"I do," she said, and then she paused for a few seconds in a way that seemed deliberate. "Hey, you mind if we go on a side quest? I have to re-up." She held up two fingers and drew them towards and away from her lips in a Smoking Weed motion.

I nodded. I felt torn about this adventure, but I knew better than to believe Sidney was asking my opinion. "Yeah, sure."

"It shouldn't be too long," she said. "I typed it in before I picked you up. It's only supposed to be, like, 10 minutes out of the way. Plus, there's nobody on the roads right now.

There's never anybody on the roads here, I thought to myself. "So, who's all coming?" I asked.

"Fuck if I know." Sidney's attention was torn between me, the road, and the GPS on her phone, which had directed us off of the main street we'd been traveling down and onto a gravel road that seemed to lead off into the middle of nowhere. "There are a couple of new people. Tom is bringing one of his friends, I think."

"More old dudes!"

Sidney laughed. "More old dudes. Tom's a good guy, though, so whatever. Plus, a bunch of people couldn't come this year, so the more the merrier. It always falls into place, right?"

I nodded. This was the fourth year Sidney was putting on Taco House. It had originally started as a fun excuse for myself and a few of our friends to stay in Sidney's childhood home for a week or so while her parents were away for the summer. The designation of "festival" was mostly tongue-in-cheek, a way of legitimizing our annual long weekend of debauchery. But over the years, most of the people from our nearby college town had gone off to grad school or followed jobs and relationships to other cities, gradually replacing the original friends-only crowd with friends of friends and people Sidney had met since graduating college—including, yes, some older dudes. One of the only constants has been the festival's name: Taco House, after Sidney's geriatric cat. But despite all of the changes over the years, the festival had managed to maintain its original spirit as an engine of friendship and spiritual rejuvenation, which was a testament to the kind of company Sidney kept.

"Is Ant coming?"

Sidney shook her head. "I invited him," she said, her sudden lack of enthusiasm revealing the existence of additional layers she didn't wish to disclose.

"Fair enough," I said.

Sidney squinted at the gravel road ahead of us, her stare piercing and hard. For a moment, you could see the disappointment bubbling up and escaping through her usual veil of nonchalance. She reached for her coffee as if in some frantic effort to occupy her hands and took a long, slow sip. When she drew the travel mug away from her lips, her face was different, sanitized of any bitterness. "I wouldn't be able to entertain him anyway. There are too many people coming."

"Fair enough," I said again, and that was that.

"Plan for tonight is we re-up on beer and stuff, and then Tom is getting here later with Jay and they're staying here tonight."

"Jay?"

"Other old dude."

"Ah."

"Everyone else is getting in tomorrow, so I don't know. We'll entertain them."

I nodded. The gravel road was lined with long, winding driveways that led to these huge, rustic-looking houses, each situated a few hundred feet apart. It was similar to the neighborhood where Sidney lived, only hers was somehow even more in the middle of nowhere.

Sidney continued, "It'll be good. I mean, I've met both of them. Well, sort of."

"You've met Tom."

"Right, and Tom buys his edibles from Jay, so I kind of know him."

I rolled my eyes, grinning a little. "So, Jay lives up this way?"

"Oh! No, no," she clarified, "I just told him to bring the edibles over later tonight. This is someone else." As she said this, she squinted back and forth between her phone and the road ahead of us. "And it should be coming right up here in a second."

We reached the end of the road, and Sidney pulled into the final driveway, which led up a small slope toward what was, by far, the largest house in the vicinity.

"Should be it," she said, pulling around in front of the house and shutting off the car.

A quick survey of my surroundings revealed that Sidney's was the only car currently parked in the driveway. I felt relieved for a minute, thinking to myself that maybe Sidney had miscalculated, maybe this mysterious semi-rural drug dealer wasn't at home right now and I wouldn't have to meet him. We would turn the car around and return to civilization, and Sidney would stop at a Dunkin' Donuts and I could get a sandwich. But just as I began to think these things, Sidney looked up from her phone and said, "So, he's home. He said we can just walk in."

I took a particularly long swig of my coffee. The plant in my chest was going to have to perk up a little faster than anticipated.

YOUNG BULL

My stomach growled as I followed Sidney to the front door of the drug dealer's house, a profound reminder that we hadn't stopped for breakfast since I'd gotten off the train. It didn't look like we would do so any time soon, either. We were out in the sticks.

When we made it to the front step, she said, "I guess we just go in," and shrugged as she pulled open the door. I followed her in, letting the storm door hiss shut behind me as we stepped forward into the foyer. A few feet ahead of us, a staircase led up to the second floor whose hallway overlooked us by way of a balcony. A giant, ornate-looking light fixture hung from the second-floor ceiling, casting yellow light on the white tiled floor where we stood. It was the kind of house everyone's family seemed to have in movies—the kind that was always played off as a normal house where normal people lived, the kind we all accepted as typical growing up, despite never knowing anyone who lived in this sort of house in real life. This was the house they built to justify the one in *Home Alone*.

"Just come in," called a voice from somewhere off to our left, and I followed Sidney into the living room. On the leather sectional was a figure that more resembled a high school kid than any drug dealer I'd seen or imagined. He was lounging with his back to us in a pair of black basketball shorts and an old white t-shirt and held up a hand as if to say, "Hold on a sec." We stood behind the couch, watching him finish his video game on the large TV that was mounted on the opposite wall. This entire situation was approaching its limit of ridiculousness. I tried to shoot a meaningful look in Sidney's direction, but she was enraptured by the game, wearing this absurdly neutral expression even as the guy on the couch began cursing someone out via the headset. A few seconds later, the game ended, and he removed the headset with an exasperated sigh.

"Is that FIFA?" I asked, trying to inject some normalcy into this moment by saying something casual, relatable.

"It's Madden," replied the mysterious figure in a tone devoid of all patience. He stood up and walked around the left side of the couch toward Sidney and me. Now that I could see his entire face, it was obvious that he was either an extremely young-looking college kid or an actual high-schooler. His mouse-brown hair curled cheesily in front of his forehead, clashing with the patches of mustache/beard hair clustered in seemingly random areas on the bottom half of his face.

Sidney nodded toward him. "Hey, Nick," she said.

He nodded back at her before turning his attention to me, grinning in amusement when he noticed my expression. "Yeah, I'm a young bull," he said. He smirked and added, "Sixteen," as if challenging me to ask any number of follow-up questions.

"Yeah, but he knows his shit," Sidney interjected, continuing to maintain her inappropriate level of neutrality.

"And you live here by yourself?" I asked. I was taking the bait, but I couldn't help myself.

"Nah," said Nick, "My mom's away until Sunday. Have the place to myself." He gestured proudly around him. My eyes scanned the room, lingering on the modern-looking glass coffee table strewn with empty plates, cans of beer and soda, and all manner of paraphernalia: a bong; a milligram scale; a turtle-shaped votive holder that he'd been using as an ashtray, overflowing with roaches and what looked like the burnt-out half of a cigar. It was the kind of thing only a sixteen-year-old drug dealer would consider Nice Digs.

"Nice," I lied.

"I have to pee," Sidney said.

I tried to give her this look like, *what are you doing? Why are you leaving me alone with this person? Why is this person a child?* But I seemed to be off our radar.

I winced through my hunger pangs as Nick and I stood alone in the living room, the Madden theme continuing to play in infuriatingly short loops on the screen behind us. We both started playing on our phones. Sidney leaving the room had dissolved any connection he and I had with each other, and we adopted the behavior of total strangers, regarding each other the way we would in public as if both of us were waiting for the same bus or something. I suspected he was watching Instagram stories, given the short bursts of loud audio playing out of his phone at regular intervals. The minutes were long. I was shamelessly avoiding eye contact, but every time my eyes drifted from my screen, I noticed he was taking small peeks at me out of the corner of his eye. He had a slimy demeanor to him, his lips perma-curled into this smug grin apropos of nothing. As this thought occurred to me, I considered whether it was inappropriate to be making this kind of judgment about somebody who wasn't even a legal adult. Then again, it couldn't possibly be appropriate to be purchasing drugs from somebody who wasn't even a legal adult, so the point seemed moot.

A few seconds later, Nick suddenly looked up from his phone and said, "I'm hungry. You hungry?" and then walked off toward what I assumed was the kitchen. I followed suit, due in larger part to the vague potential of scoring some food than to any notion of wanting to spend even more time alone with him. The kitchen was similar to the rest of the house: high-ceilinged and modern, its many surfaces strewn with Nick's teen-boy detritus. He made his way over to an area where the spoils of his latest stoned grocery run seemed to have been piled, pushing aside a few near-empty bags of chips and pretzels to procure a dented box of Pop-Tarts from underneath. Primal desperation welled up in me as I watched him tear open the thin, silver wrapper, pulling out a single iced strawberry pastry before handing the package to me.

"Thanks," I said, trying and failing to slow my roll as I ripped the remaining Pop-Tart from the wrapper. I took a large bite and barely chewed, gulping to force the large, crumbly bits of dry crust down my throat.

Nick nodded, and we stood in the kitchen in silence, each working on our Pop-Tarts. It was a utilitarian kind of silence. Having been fed, I felt less irritated by Nick's presence and proximity, but my hunger outweighed my disinterest in conversation.

Halfway through my Pop-Tart, I said, "My mom would only buy the non-frosted Pop-Tarts when I was a kid. I always thought they were so bad."

"Oh," said Nick. He didn't look up from his phone.

"Yeah."

"I didn't even know they made those," he said.

"Yeah, they do," I said.

Before I could elaborate, Nick opened another Instagram story, flooding the echoey kitchen with some kind of loud, distorted yelling. I winced. It was the closest I could get as opposed to rolling my eyes without feeling rude.

Despite my distaste for him, there was some stubborn part of me that wanted him to find me relatable or cool. That alone was uncomfortable enough to make me eager to leave. I'd never anticipated being the kind of adult who tried so hard to win the approval of The Youth, and I didn't enjoy having this part of me exposed this early in the day. Since leaving wasn't an option, I would have to get him to talk to me.

"So, you're in school?" I asked.

"Yeah," Nick said.

"Cool, cool."

"College after?" I was thinking to myself that it might be silly of me to ask a drug dealer if he planned on going to college after high school, but then I thought to myself that maybe it was wrong of me to assume that a drug dealer didn't have any aspirations besides selling drugs for the rest of his life.

For the first and only time since we'd entered his house, Nick lit up. "Yeah," he said, strangely sincere.

I smiled back, relieved. "To study what?"

"Business."

Before I could ask any further questions, Sidney re-entered the kitchen, and Nick and I snapped into place like a pair of employees whose supervisor had just appeared, our eyes no longer repelling each other as we both watched her fiddle around in her wallet.

"Here's 60," she said, nodding to Nick as she held out a few bills.

"Sweet, alright," Nick said, and he led the two of us back into the living room.

I leaned against the couch. Nick handed Sidney a small Tupperware container with a bag of weed in it, which she shoved in the bag she was wearing.

"Thanks," she said.

"Yeah, thanks," I echoed.

Nick nodded up at us in acknowledgment, shoving the bills in his pocket. "So," he asked, "when's the thing start?"

"Thing?" I asked.

Nick nodded. "Sid said there was some kind of festival, something like that. Tacos and something?"

"Ah, yeah, yeah, yeah, yeah," Sidney said, taking the reins and leaving me to ruminate hopelessly on Nick's casual delivery of that nickname. "It's tonight. Well, we have a couple of guys getting here. But it's just going to be lowkey, not really a thing."

"Sounds like a thing. It's just you and them?" His scummy smirk had returned and was now directed squarely at Sidney, who rolled her eyes.

"Don't be gross."

"Nah, I'm just saying, for real, be careful," he said, looking at each of us in turn with the world's least convincing eye contact.

"We can handle it," Sidney chirped, digging in her bag for her keys. I could tell as she was gathering herself to leave the house that she had finally reached her limit with him, but her exasperation was a lot more playful than mine. She gave me a look that said we were done here, and I nodded back.

"It was good meeting you," I said, tossing my head over my shoulder as I walked away.

"Yeah, same here," he said, returning to his position on the couch.

I felt a wave of relief as we crossed from the living room into the foyer. He hadn't bothered to see us out, but I preferred it that way. Sidney's keys jingled in her opposite hand as she fumbled with the knob. We were moving quickly, relieved of the burden of Nick and his awkward line of questioning.

As soon as the front door clicked shut behind us, she turned to me, laughing. "What the fuck?"

"I don't know!" I said. "Is he always like that?"

"I mean, yeah, but I think he turned it up a notch. Probably since you were there."

"And you left me alone with him!" I hissed. I opened the car door and slid into the passenger seat. I took a quick swig of my coffee, thankfully still warm.

"I know, I know," Sidney said. "He's harmless though. He's just...you know."

"Sixteen?"

"Yeah." Sidney didn't look up to see my look of disbelief. She turned the key in the ignition, and we set off down the long driveway. "You hungry?" she asked. "There's that Chinese place."

THE BOTTOM OF A HOLE

After we ordered the Chinese takeout, we had to smoke weed. It was a whole thing with Sidney, she never wanted to eat anything and had to smoke weed before meals so she'd have an appetite. I obliged, even knowing smoking would make the wait feel even longer and I was already starving. We were on the couch in Sidney's parents' living room playing music on the TV. Her parents had a projector screen that you could use to play videos from a computer, and during Taco House we'd use it to queue up songs on her laptop so they'd play over the big speakers. Sidney grabbed her bag from next to the arm of the couch and took out the weed we'd bought from Nick.

"You think it's actually good?" I asked. I knew nothing about weed or what would constitute Good Weed. I smoked casually and never bought it on my own. Sidney knew this, but it was something to say, so I said it.

"Usually is, from him," she said. She reached toward the coffee table, sliding over this little tray where she kept all of her paraphernalia, the contents neatly sequestered for easy, inconspicuous cleanup. It was the more organized Adult equivalent of the drug-littered table in Nick's living room.

I watched her pinch small clumps of the weed between her thumb and finger and place them in a grinder before packing the bowl. Sitting there in her white romper, assembling the herb, she looked wise, centered in this way that had always been lost on me. I was watching a ritual. She lit the bowl and took a hit before handing it off to me. Not entirely sure how to light it, I took my hit quickly to mooch off hers. I got only the scraps, which felt right—taking the pathetic little plume of smoke into my mouth, not my lungs, even. Just enough.

Once we were sufficiently stoned, Sidney got up and retrieved the bag of takeout from the counter. "General Tso's," she said, handing me a plastic container with *TSO* written in Sharpie across the lid. She pulled out the other large container and placed it in front of her spot at the coffee table.

"What did you get?" I asked. I popped the plastic lid off of the container in front of me and dug in my fork, trying to evenly coat everything in the sauce. There was a little red chili wedged into the corner, half wrapped around a floret of broccoli. Looking at it, I suddenly realized it was still technically morning. My first meal of the day was going to be a Chinese takeout meal with a spicy pepper in it. Unless you counted the Pop-Tart I had been so graciously given by Sidney's 16-year-old dealer who could barely put FIFA down long enough to complete the transaction. The point was that so much had happened, and none of it was normal. This was the whole conceit of Taco House, what someone like Sidney would refer to as the Magic in it. The chicken and broccoli squelched around my fork as I slid the pepper around the container.

"Some sesame tofu thing." She pulled the lid off of her box. "I don't know. It looks good though."

We were quiet as we ate. It was nice to not be having a conversation. To not be On. Historically, Taco House weekends tended to provide few, if any, of these moments, so I was trying to soak it in: the TV playing one of those lo-fi hip-hop beats channels at a low volume, the squelching of our food and the forks scraping along the bottom, plastic on plastic. All of it slow in all of the right ways. I fantasized that Tom and the others weren't coming, that the whole weekend was just going to be this. Maybe each of them was suddenly dealing with their family emergency—nothing serious or fatal, just something that made them busy. In two minutes, one of those old guys would text Sidney and let her know to call it off. It was all falling into place.

Sidney got up to do something—I didn't know what. I was focused on the TV, which was playing this slowed-down GIF of a teenage girl drawn in an anime style studying in her bedroom.

Every few seconds she would look away from her notebook and take a sip of tea, and when she would put it down the surface of the tea would slosh around but never quite spill over the rim of the mug. Then, she would turn back to her book, holding the corner of the page as if preparing to flip it but then never actually doing so, her eyes squinting and scanning back and forth across the page. The longer I watched, the more other details I noticed. There was a box fan propped up near a stack of papers, making the corners flap around in the wind, and an empty glass bottle with a bendy straw sitting on the floor beside the bed.

I began obsessively speculating about the origin of this little animation and the many others commonly deployed on these YouTube channels. I imagined a database of anime GIFs curated for this specific purpose. A guy decides he wants to start a 24/7 radio station on YouTube and purchases a month's worth of access to this large repository of looping animations. Scrolling through their catalog is like peering at a cross-section of a little dollhouse: each tile another dimly-lit cartoon room containing a different color coffee mug or desk chair or curtain. In each room, a different schoolgirl flipping pages in a book and never seeming to make any progress. It sounds cynical, but there's a lot hidden in these seemingly-minor differences. Selecting the correct scene is a precise art that can't be rushed. You might scroll for hours in search of some particular feeling.

Sidney came back into the room holding a bottle of water. "I put your food in the fridge with mine," she said. "Yours is on top."

She was standing behind the couch, leaning on the doorway, but her voice sounded like it was coming from outside. I nodded.

She sat down beside me and stared at the screen for maybe a millisecond. A length of time inadequate for appreciating the subtle flash of anguish on the schoolgirl's face in the first frame after she pulls the teacup away from her mouth. "What do you think?" I didn't typically find Sidney irritating, but in these circumstances, both her proximity and her volume felt offensive to me, and I winced. "Is it hitting?"

"Hitting?" I was at the bottom of a hole, attempting a self-taught crash course in English solely to respond to this question.

"Yeah," she said. "You seem like you're really feeling it."

"Oh," I said. Weed. "Yeah, it's hitting good." It didn't feel like a sentence I would ever say, but there it was, flapping in the wind like a piece of T.P. trapped in a waistband.

"Good." She smirked. "It seems stupid, but Nick really does know what he's doing. I wouldn't fuck with him otherwise."

"Mm," I said.

I looked down at my hands, curling and uncurling my fingers in a sort of squeezing motion. They felt numb like I'd been sitting on them or holding them in a weird position, but I was almost completely certain that I'd just been sitting normally. Maybe it was possible to lose the feeling in your hands from being too high. If so, hopefully, it wasn't a permanent thing. I turned my attention back to the video. My thoughts were heading in a non-ideal direction, and I needed to yank on the leash.

"You good?" Sidney asked. "You seem lost or something."

I turned to her, trying to reassure her with eye contact, some look to let her know I was present and accounted for. But her face was deeply overstimulating; all of her features were so pronounced and real they were an existential threat. This heavy, wasting feeling had begun to spread from the center of my chest to each of my limbs like her concern was physically shriveling me. There was no question now: I was losing it.

I don't know exactly what I looked like at this moment—frozen, most likely, judging by my mounting feeling of certainty that I was in the process of leaving my body for the night and possibly forever. Something about my demeanor signaled to

Sidney that I needed rescuing. In an instant, her concern hardened into urgency. She reached for my legs and pivoted me to a reclining position on the couch. "Alright, we're going to lay you down," she asserted. She left no room for me to object or even attempt the work of twisting my own body lengthwise, although, by this point, I wasn't capable of either. I was stickied to the skylight, involuntarily astral projecting above Sidney's childhood living room. "I'll be right back, okay? I'm just getting you water." The girl lying on the couch nodded weakly as Sidney walked away.

I was on the ceiling, watching her breathe and her chest move. This wasn't the first time I'd had this sort of thing happen to me. I'd certainly Greened Out before. I'd had my moments. But this time, I felt acutely aware of the difference in circumstances. The other times this had happened, the other times I'd been reduced to The Girl On The Couch and was forced to watch myself come to from the ceiling, I'd had an anchor, some vague understanding that I was taken care of. It was weird to hear myself think this. Wasn't Sidney taking care of me? Wasn't her presence in the house and the sounds of her filling a glass with water concrete proof that I was not fending for myself alone? It should have been, but it wasn't. Because I'd never needed people like Sidney for that. There was always a love interest, a "home" person, even if just a familiar string of characters on my screen telling me that they loved me and would see me soon. I'd certainly felt alone during those times, but as I watched the girl struggle to prop herself up against the arm of the couch, I realized that *now* was the moment in which I was truly untethered. Depending on the kindness of a friend who could just as easily have made light of the whole thing and told me to snap out of it. Friends aren't supposed to make you feel that way, but they always did. There was the person I loved, and then there was everyone else. And now that I didn't have a person to love, anything could happen.

When the girl finished drinking her water, I shifted my body on the couch, so I was facing forward again, reoriented toward the TV. The lo-fi channel was still on and looping that same GIF of the girl studying and nearly spilling her tea. Sidney hadn't bothered to turn it off during my Episode which made it seem shorter and less significant than it had felt for me, and this was a huge kindness. Upon observing my newfound second wind, Sidney walked back toward the kitchen again, yelling over her shoulder, "What is it with Chinese food? I always eat, like, two bites, feel full, put it away, and then, like, ten minutes later I'm starving." Then came the familiar sounds of the fridge opening and closing, the takeout container popping open, the microwave as it hummed and beeped. It was as if the whole scene was speaking in perfect unison, *The night's not ruined. Everything can go back to normal.* And it wasn't, and for the next few hours, everything did.

We were on the couch watching a Vine compilation when the guys called. Tom and his friend were about 40 minutes out and they wanted to know if we needed anything besides the edibles. Sidney told them to pick up some liquor. They could use their best judgment on what kind or how much, and besides, there was plenty here already, to begin with. I considered jokingly, and then a bit more seriously, asking the guys to pick up some actual food for the weekend so that we didn't die of dehydration or malnutrition or scurvy from subsiding on liquor and edibles alone for days on end. Sidney had already drawn the conversation to a close, though, and placed her phone on the coffee table with a sharp little sigh.

"Well," she said. "Guess it's happening."

"Yep," I said. I looked around the now dimly-lit room, trying to pin and preserve for posterity the final moments of calm. Like how in the middle of winter when you're hating your life and scraping snow off your car you wish you could bottle just a bit of it for that day in August when you're drenched in sweat the second you dry off from the shower. There would be calm again eventually, of course, but by the time it came, I would have forgotten all about this dread and be naively wishing for something to happen.

"We should get our shit together, huh?"

I sighed. "Yeah."

Sidney and I had barely moved from the living room since we'd arrived. My bag was still propped up by the stairs, where I'd carelessly thrown it hours prior in an eagerness to get something to eat. Luckily, the bulk of my Greening Out sensation had subsided, but it'd left behind this hazy undercurrent that had sapped any interest in moving or activity. Something had to change before people started arriving, or I would be completely hopeless. It took all of the motivation I had left to lift myself from the couch and lumber toward the stairs. "I'm going to shower, I think," I said.

"Okay, that works. I'm gonna stick around down here and get everything together. Towels are in the closet."

"Cool."

RANSOM

By the time I got out of the shower, I could already hear the guys talking downstairs. There was Tom's voice, which I'd heard a few times before in passing, and another, burlier one, which I assumed was his yet-to-be-identified friend. He was the only one loud enough to make out words with any clarity. Something about the house and how he'd driven past it many times before, obviously not knowing it was the home of such a strange and insular event. Even with the blow dryer running, the man's booming laughter phased through the ceiling and floor to the bottoms of my feet. It occurred to me that maybe my brief episode of Greening Out had been a blessing all along, leaving behind a slight fog that downgraded the vibrations into only a minor annoyance.

I'd learned from my many experiences taking too long to get dressed for family gatherings that there was no graceful way to arrive late to a party from elsewhere in the house. No matter what you were wearing or doing or who else had or hadn't already arrived and what they were wearing or doing, you had to descend the stairs in front of everybody. It was a kind of performance: A Big Reveal. It was that scene in *The Princess Diaries* where Anne Hathaway has to practice her entrance for the big state dinner but ends up getting a man's sleeve on fire and trying in vain to smother it in an ice bucket. Only instead of gliding down the stairs in a beautiful gown tailored precisely to my body shape, it was this boxy t-shirt dress I'd gotten off the clearance rack at Gabe's up in Erie. I felt the weight of what was to come as I crossed from the second floor onto the first, passing that point where second-floor walls concealed the stairs and, by extension, me, traipsing down the stairs in this kind of D-list outfit I already regretted.

"Hey!" Sidney bellowed from the couch. It wasn't in her nature to deny me a grand entrance.

The guys looked up, beers in hand, and I nodded at them in a way that I hoped looked cool but most likely did not.

"There she is!" Tom said as I entered the living room. I didn't know him super well, but he had this smarmy way of talking, this lilt to his voice that made everything sound ironic. "Beer's on the table."

Tom motioned toward his friend, and they both slid over to make room for me on the couch. I kept to the far end, attaching myself to the sofa arm out of some weird paranoia about touching thighs. I reached for the half-finished six-pack in the center of the coffee table and pulled out a bottle. There was an air of spectacle as I lifted the hem of my dress slightly, revealing the world's smallest sliver of upper thigh as I wrapped it around the bottle for leverage. When the cap came unscrewed, it went flying, clattering onto the table in front of me. I straightened my dress and made some kind of noise, fumbling for the cap as it spun around on the glass surface.

I kept my eyes forward, deliberately watching Sidney as she talked about the highways Tom and his friend had taken to get to the house. They were looking at me, that was a fact. Not in a creepy way, at least not one I cared to prove or acknowledge. It wasn't some kind of distrust for them that made me wary. I just hated the knowledge of it, this awareness of being perceived, maybe, as this new, shiny thing. It had this way of infecting me and making it feel impossible to just do anything. And then, the worst part, pretending you didn't notice it, that their eyes on you didn't chip away at your subjective being. What if I made some half-joke and they denied it, made me seem like a narcissist for expecting their attention? I thought of all of this, watching Sidney talk with their hands and the guys drink their beers.

"What?" I whipped my head to my right, where Tom had been trying to ask me a question.

"Do you know Jay?" he gestured at his friend.

"Oh," I said. "No."

Jay was already looking at me when I met his eyes. They were big and round and wet, like a dog's. I believe in souls—as in, I think humans have them—but most of the time people just seemed like bodies. Either there was nothing in there or it was all fused. For practical purposes, they were just one entity, a single Thing. Jay had that rare quality about him where you could tell there was something in there: a hard line where the packaging stopped and the contents began. Like you could slide a spatula between them and pry him out of him in one damp layer, like a fried egg. It's not that nobody in this room had anything else to them—Sidney did, we all did—but Jay gave off the distinct impression of being a passenger in a vessel. I could see him looking at me through the cutouts in the costume.

"Hey," I said.

"Hello, hello," said Jay. He held up his beer like a weird little salute and added, "Taco House."

"Taco House," I replied, just to say something.

"Did you come from out of town?" He gestured at my still-wet hair as if trying to connect those two things.

"Only the city, so not really."

"Me too."

"Cool." I threw back a good third of my beer just to buy myself some time to respond with something conducive to good conversation.

"How do you know Sidney?"

"College."

Jay nodded. "Nice."

"What about you?"

He ran his hand from the front of his head to the back. Jay was as close as you could get to bald without actually being bald, and as his hand moved you could see the uniformly-short, dark bristles bend gently against his palm.

"I don't, really," he said, laughing a little. "I know Tom."

"I don't know Tom. I don't even know how Sidney knows Tom."

For the first time since I'd come downstairs, Jay and I shared a genuine laugh. Tom and Sidney had splintered off from our conversation and had begun gradually drifting toward the kitchen as Sidney told some story about being mistaken for a minor in the liquor store. She was throwing up her hands, Tom was laughing. Jay and I sat there quietly for a few seconds, drinking, trying to size them up through subtle glances. It wasn't inconceivable that the two of them liked each other, that after the night wore on and the beers ran out something would happen there. Then Jay and I would be stuck sitting together on Sidney's mom's couch while I tried not to talk about my breakup. Jay dreaded the thought, and it showed. Whatever his intention, though, it didn't offend me. We were effectively strangers, and his expression led me to believe that his frustration was less with having to talk to me and more with being abandoned by Tom in an unfamiliar place, the latest in what was likely a string of instances in which Jay had been forced to tag along with him so he could spend time with some girl. Or maybe this was all a projection of my own feelings at this moment, and it *was* me he was sitting there dreading. Maybe he could sense the break-up on me, could see it oozing from my pores like a green, stinking mist.

"I think they met at a show," Jay said.

"Oh yeah, true."

Sidney was always going to these little house shows in town. It was her primary Thing, the very cloth from which this weekend was ambitiously cut. The fliers would get posted on Facebook a few days beforehand, listing a lineup of all of these little local bands that were just different combinations of the same 10 or 12 guys in the scene. The crowd was usually made up of the guys who weren't performing, their girlfriends, the bands' girlfriends, a rotating cast of all of their friends, an overzealous guy trying to elbow his way into the scene and asking everyone who makes eye contact with to come over and Jam, and usually a few wildcards who were genuinely just there for the music. Sometimes Sidney would drag me to one of these shows, and I would spend the whole night standing against the wall, not talking to anyone. It was like being at a party where everyone knew each other and looked at you like an over-eager freak if you tried to butt in. And yet, somehow, Sidney seemed to meet a lot of random people at these things. I didn't know how she did it.

Decidedly out of things to say, Jay leaned forward on the couch and called out to Sidney in the kitchen. "You have any wine?"

"I don't think so," she yelled back from the kitchen doorway. "My parents might have some. I can check downstairs?"

Tom and Jay shared a look, and Jay laughed.

"What?" she asked.

Jay blew air out of his nose and looked down into his beer with a smirk. "I was saying to Tom on the way here that there was no way this was your actual house."

"Why not?"

"Besides the fact that there's no way you have a mortgage at, like, 21?"

He looked up at Tom, who responded with a strangled, uncomfortable chuckle.

"It just doesn't look like a 21-year-old's place. They all look the same."

"Do not!" said Sidney. She was leaning in the doorway with her hip cocked, a pose too coy to be an accident, but, knowing her, probably was.

"Visit a lot of 21-year-olds, do you?" I butted in, half to diffuse the tension and half to just get a line in and stop feeling awkward.

"He wishes," Tom said, and he and Sidney laughed.

I turned to look at Jay. He swallowed the last of his drink, his grin itself the line between embarrassment and mirth—the way someone looks when they wipe out in public in a slapstick way, and the pride overshadows the bruise. I felt like an ass.

Sidney disappeared into the basement, Tom trailing uselessly behind her. Jay and I were essentially alone now, listening to them banter like perfect foils as they descended. There was nothing left in my bottle, so I pulled out my phone, something to hold. I opened Messenger and tapped Cody's name. It was instinct, and it was disappointing. I thought so little about us and yet was somehow preoccupied, trapped in the routine of wondering what he was doing and telling him when things happened. I scrolled up through a week or so of conversation, not reading, not typing, like a nicotine addict miming the act of lighting the cigarette and holding it to his lips.

"Hot date or something?" It was what had become Jay's typical sardonic tone, an edge I wasn't yet sure if I liked.

I laughed it off. "No, just checking stuff, you know."

He blew air out of his nose and set down his bottle on the table to free his hands. *"Hey, I'm stuck at a party with this creepy old dude. Can you come pick me up?"* A vaguely bitter grin spread across his face as he moved his thumbs in a mock-typing motion. *"They don't even have tacos here."*

"This isn't a party," I teased, shrugging.

Jay let his mouth hang open in fake disgrace. "Tell me how you really feel." He snorted. "Damn."

"Oh, come on. Fine." I locked my phone and set it performatively on the table, rolling my eyes.

"No, no, it's fine. Text your boyfriend. I'm just being an ass."

"Funny you say that."

"Why? He on his way here to fight me?"

"We broke up, like, two days ago."

"Oh, well I'm...sorry?"

"Nah," I said. "Don't be."

"Oh. Well, alright."

When I'd dropped the bomb, I'd expected him to take an interest, to ask questions, make it about him somehow. With most guys, there was this vibe you were being consumed like if they drained you there'd be tea leaves to read at the bottom. But Jay sat there silently, requesting zero slack and taking, somehow, even less. Without normal urgency, it was hard to gauge his interest. Either he was this blank, ambivalent to know me, or this was all part of the plan somehow: a word-vomit-inducing silence. If so, it was working.

"We were together for a few years."

"How many is a few?"

"Four? Five?"

"Long enough," Jay answered as if to correct me. He turned his attention toward the basement door for a split second, seemingly expecting Sidney and Tom to re-emerge at any moment.

I smiled. "Long enough."

"Apparently." I attempted a laugh but only managed a pointed exhale. "Yeah. Anyway, he's not coming."

"I get the sense that you don't really want him to."

"You mean you get the sense that I'm the one that broke up with him."

"No," Jay said. "I mean that I get the sense that you don't really want him to come here."

"Are you doing something?"

"Doing something?"

"Like," I looked to the side, away from Jay and whatever face he was making, "trying something."

Jay laughed softly, tilting the bottle to his lips as he threw up his other hand in a half-shrug. One ill-advised peek at his eyes and I could tell he was holding back a torrent of sarcasm and ridicule.

"I don't know!"

"Well, for what it's worth, I'm not that passive-aggressive."

"Well," was all I said.

Jay and I were rescued by the sound of Tom and Sidney's banter floating up from the basement, growing louder as they reached the top of the stairs and pushed the door open.

"God," said Tom, "who died?"

Sidney shot a look to Tom over her shoulder. Her expression was one I recognized—open-mouthed, as manic as it was awed. Something had already managed to happen between the two of them. In the few moments we'd each been left to our own devices, she'd managed to win his attention, and I'd somehow tainted things with Jay beyond repair.

My eyes followed the bottle as Tom set it down on the table in front of Jay and me.

"It's called 'Ransom,'" Sidney said, her entire body pivoted in a way that suggested Tom was the only other sentient being in the room. "It's just, like, a blend or something."

"Red blend," said Jay to no one in particular, spinning it around for a better look at the label.

"Seems alright," I added.

"You guys can open it," Sidney said. "Here." Her small hand reached down and clasped the neck of the bottle, yanking away our only viable shot at a conversation.

Tom leaned against the kitchen doorway, watching as Sidney stood on her toes to grab some glasses from a high cupboard. "How far back does it go?" He pointed out the kitchen window at the abyss quickly darkening at the edge of the backyard.

"Oh," Sidney's voice echoed off the cabinet walls. "It's, like, acres."

"Damn."

"Yeah. But it's mostly just wooded. We cut a trail through it back in high school, but it's probably overgrown by now. We used to have parties."

"So why are we having a funeral in the living room instead of a forest party?"

Jay snorted.

Sidney emerged from the cabinet, her fingers curled around the stems of four smudged glasses. "It's overgrown like I said." The glasses clanked against each other, wobbling precariously as she set them on the counter.

"You tease!"

Sidney fake-scoffed, turning and yanking the cork in one fluid motion. The opener flew out of her hand, clattering on the floor and sliding across the kitchen to Tom's feet. "Sorry. Accident."

"Oh, don't be modest."

Whether to offset the mounting sexual tension or just to weigh in, Jay piped up suddenly. "I'd go."

"Seriously?" I said.

Jay shrugged. "I was a boy scout."

Sidney sighed, handing Jay and I each a glass. "It has to be tonight if you really want to. I don't want to keep track of a dozen people in the woods."

"Wait," Tom said. "Edibles first?"

"Shit." Sidney had barely swallowed her first sip of wine before replying. "Yeah. Let's do it." She gestured to Tom, who gestured to me.

I reached into the bag nestled against the side of the couch, rifling through until I felt plastic crinkling. It was one of those thick, gallon-sized plastic baggies, stuffed with ten or so brownies.

"These them?" I asked.

"There's another bag in the car," Jay said. "I brought this one for tonight."

"There's a dozen in here."

Jay shrugged. "I make 'em a dozen at a time."

"Well, I'm probably not going to have one."

"You don't partake?"

"I'd—"

"She Greened Out earlier," Sidney interrupted.

"I'm fine. I just needed to eat something."

"That's rough," Jay tried to interject, but I blew him off.

"I guess. I'm just gonna lay off for tonight."

"Well," said Jay, "if you change your mind, there are three huge ones with your name on it." He held out his arm for the bag, and I handed it off. The soft hairs on his arms grazed the top of my thigh as he pulled away.

"Yeah," I said, "thanks."

"So, we're going then," said Tom.

"Yeah," Sidney said. "You bringing the wine?"

I stood up fast enough for the blood to rush out of my head, wobbling as I squeezed past Jay and moved toward the kitchen. "I'll hold it." There was only one thing that would get me through this pseudo-double-date of an evening, and I wanted full access.

There were a collective clinking and rustling of drinks being picked up and placed down, jackets being shrugged on and zipped up. I curled my fingers harder around the neck of the half-drunk Ransom.

"Mind if I have a cigarette real quick?" came the sound of Tom's voice from behind me.

"Yeah, on the porch. I'll come with." Sidney pulled her jacket the rest of the way up her shoulder as she rushed behind him, their steps painfully in-sync.

"I'll meet you guys out there," I said, my voice trailing off as the back door sealed shut with a hiss.

"Don't hog the Ransom," came Jay's voice from behind me.

I flinched a bit, my fingers slipping a bit down the neck of the bottle. I whipped around to face Jay and secured the bottom with my other palm. "Well, you guys have the edibles."

"Right." He smirked. "You're still wobbly."

"Wobbly?"

"Yeah, from earlier. The Greening Out?"

"Yeah." I looked down. "I guess." Sidney's laughter drifted into the kitchen through one of the open windows, inflicting a painful awareness of how long we'd been standing there in limbo, keeping them waiting.

"What happened?"

"I don't know," I said. "I had to lay down for a while. It wasn't that big of a deal."

"Anxiety. It happens."

"Yeah." I yanked the cork from the bottle and occupied myself with a long draw.

Over the bridge of my nose, I could see a small smile spread across Jay's face, betraying the current vibe of our small talk which bordered on adversarial. When I moved the bottle away from my face, he had his hand out, beckoning for a sip. I passed the bottle.

"Thank you kindly," Jay replied, divorced from his typical manner of speaking. His voice had a sing-song lilt to it as if he'd suddenly transformed into a slightly-dweeby radio DJ: a small glimpse of the part of himself he'd been masking in brusqueness. I laughed, but it was a friendly laugh. Genuine. Jay took a hefty sip of the wine, sighing as it went down.

THE CALL OF THE VOID

"Do you think they're still waiting for us?" I looked over my shoulder at the kitchen door through which Tom and Sidney had disappeared. Neither of them was visible by now, though their voices still occasionally floated in from somewhere out of view.

Jay handed back the bottle, smiling, a glint of mischief in his eyes. "No way," he said. "They're out there hiding somewhere."

"Yeah," I said between sips of Ransom. "They're waiting to jump and scare us."

"Or they're making out."

"Stop!"

Jay shrugged. "It's been known to happen."

I led the way out of the kitchen and into the backyard. The smell of Tom's and Sidney's cigarettes lingered by the door, the only indication that they'd been nearby. Above us, the silhouettes of trees sliced into the blue-black of the night sky. We were far enough from the city that there were stars out—not the full-on pastoral spread, but more than the light pollution at home would ever allow me to see.

"I only get to see stars like this a few times a year. It's so stupid." The drinks I'd consumed up to this point we're beginning to take effect, loud, girly messiness beginning to make itself known. I looked behind me at Jay, watched his wide, backlit body make its way through the few meters of unkempt lawn between us. He was a slow drunk—loose but somehow composed. Maybe it was the age thing, maybe it wasn't, but either way, I was embarrassed by the contrast.

He reached a spot in the grass behind me, puffing a bit as he spoke. "I like to go on these day-long drives," he said, "through West Virginia. It's even better out there."

"I bet," I said.

Now that we'd stopped moving, I could hear the light crunching of Tom's and Sidney's footsteps somewhere up ahead where the open lawn began to converge into what must have been the small, wooded trail she had mentioned. We followed the sound, using my phone's flashlight to illuminate the ground in front of us.

Tom held out his arm before any of us had a chance to speak. "Brownies?" he asked, his smirk barely visible in the dark.

Jay reached into the ratty messenger bag he'd been carrying and removed the bag with the brownies in it. He pulled one out of the bag and placed it ceremoniously into Tom's palm, then a second brownie which he tore in two before popping the slightly larger half in his mouth. It was at this moment that I knew exactly what was coming. Jay held the other half out to me. "Change your mind?"

Tom, who had eaten his in what seemed to be a single bite, pointed with enthusiasm at the bag as he nodded at me, crumbs shifting in the corners of his mouth.

I sighed. "Alright."

"It's only half." Jay tried to further persuade me even as he passed the brownie to me.

I nodded. It was a small piece, an inch wide by maybe two inches long, but it felt dense in my hand. The taste was pleasantly surprising, not as weedy as I'd come to expect from edibles. There was that trope in TV and movies where someone would eat a brownie and have no idea there was weed in it, only to find themselves feeling inexplicably weird. I had yet to encounter a pot brownie that made that kind of plot device seem believable, but this one came the closest. I washed it down with the Ransom. Next to me, I heard the crinkling of Jay's hand as it dove back into the bag for a third brownie to hand to Sidney.

"Alright," said Jay with weird bravado. "Onward."

And we went.

"What's our destination?" I wasn't expecting much of an answer. It was just nervous chatter, just something to fill the gap before the brownie hit or there was something to say—whichever came first.

We were following Sidney's lead, now, up a slight incline. The path had narrowed, and every so often Tom would have to hold a rogue branch to keep it from recoiling into my face when he let go. I did the same for Jay, who was behind me, careful not to let our fingers brush in the handing-off.

"Not sure," came Sidney's voice from up ahead. "Gorge?"

"What's the gorge?" asked Jay.

"It's like this cliff-thing. Underneath the creek opens up into a lake sort of thing and you can climb down. It's like a watering hole."

"Why have I never been here?" I asked.

"It's more fun with more people," she said.

I was beginning to wish one of us had thought to bring some water. The sun may have gone down, but we were still walking so far and uphill and, of course, would eventually have to go back. An on-the-nose beginning to a horror movie about stupid potheads getting lost or murdered in the woods at night. In the eerie quiet you could almost hear the guy sitting on his couch screaming at us to turn back and do this in the morning. But the parts were all already in motion. All I could do now was hope that the scene would have a better ending than expected.

Another half mile or so ahead was a stretch Sidney called The Devil's Backbone. Whether or not she'd coined the name herself was never made clear, but the reasoning was. It was dark, steep, narrow, arcing over a shallow creek that ran beside it, and widened and deepened as it did. I still had the flashlight turned on, waving my phone back and forth to map out the boundaries of the cliff we were now crossing. Drunk, the brownie undoubtedly beginning to disintegrate and disperse its contents at the pit of my stomach, I was thoroughly unequipped for the task at hand. I was simultaneously aware of two things: the edge to my left that dropped off into the abyss, and the fact that it wasn't quite as narrow a path as it seemed. Drunk as I was, I hadn't exactly reached the stumbling stage. I had no reason to picture myself slipping and hurtling to my death toward a bed of sharp stones. And yet...

"This reminds me of the mall," I said.

Sidney and Tom were up further ahead, having their separate conversation, leaving Jay to coach me through this hike and hear my nervous anecdotes.

"What?" he said.

"When I was a kid and I would go to the mall, there was this giant beam that stretched across the upper floor, like, connecting the opposite edges together."

It was silent except for Jay's breathing and the Ransom now clanking around in his bag where I'd agreed to let him store it.

I continued. "I always wanted to just climb over the railing and sit on the beam. Or like, walk across." I was struggling, too, maybe even a bit more than Jay was, and had to pause to catch my breath. "Or jump off."

"The call of the void."

"What?"

"It's the name for that thing when you're up high and you have intrusive thoughts about jumping. Or wondering what it would be like to cut off your finger or hand. Floor it off the side of the bridge."

"Oh, good," I said. "So, I'm not insane."

"Never said that."

I laughed or gave the closest approximation I could under this exertion. I wasn't sure the specific border of The Devil's Backbone, but we seemed to be nearing the end of it, the steepness leveling off up ahead. The path had widened, too, into a sort of clearing where Tom and Sidney stood, waiting for us to catch up.

"Everyone thinks of putting their hand on a hot stovetop," Jay added. "We can't help it."

"Why?"

"If I could tell you that, there would be a lot of bars out of business."

"And we'd be inside right now."

"Maybe so."

When we reached Tom and Sidney, we all regrouped, our bags and jackets rustling softly in the dark as we waited for our heart rates to stabilize. Sidney gestured down to our left, and I twisted my phone for the light. As she'd promised, we'd reached the swimming hole. And this precarious overlook on which we now found ourselves was the gorge, seemingly sculpted for the express purpose of slipping, falling, and/or flinging oneself over the edge and into the dark water. But there was no way we'd be doing that. It was dark, I was nearly incapacitated, and through her façade of boundless energy and alertness, I could see Sidney was, too.

"Hope you all know how to swim," said Tom, reading my mind or somehow spiting me. "Looks deep."

"Which one of you is carrying me back home when I crack my head open against those rocks?" I asked.

"I've done this before," said Sidney, as if to step between us like some kind of verbal human shield. "Nobody is going to hit their head." She took a twig off the ground and held it over the edge of the gorge, then released it, watching it disappear into the water below. "See? We'll be fine."

I wasn't sure exactly what she'd thought she was proving with the twig, but whatever it was, she hadn't persuaded me. I laughed—part nervousness, part exasperation, hardly an iota of actual laughter. "Pretty sure I'll fall harder than a twig."

"Actually," Tom said, "you and the twig would fall at the exact same rate." When I turned my phone his way, he was inside his shirt, his head just beginning to reappear on the other side of the hem as he shrugged it off and onto the ground at his feet. "Gravity."

"That's only technically true," I said.

"She's right," said Jay. "Air molecules and wind resistance and whatever."

I twisted my head around. He was smiling, and still clothed—a sign he was potentially down to stay up there with me and not let me chicken out alone.

Sidney sighed. "There's a trail down to the bottom if you wanna walk and meet us. It's kind of grown over, though. I haven't used it." She started removing her shirt, causing Jay to quickly whip around out of modesty, or some performance of it. "Your mileage may vary."

"I mean, sure," I said. "I guess I'll meet you down there?" I looked at Jay, trying to make some kind of meaningful contact, but his eyes were still averted.

"Yeah," Sidney said. "Just keep walking past this cliff thing and follow the hill down."

"Alright," said Jay suddenly from behind me. He shot me another grin, gesturing forward as Sidney's shirt hit the grass with a barely-audible crunch.

"Alright," I said.

Once Jay and I were far enough away from the gorge, I slowed down, letting him catch up to me so I could talk without breathing so hard.

"This is stupid, right?"

Jay's laugh was warm, adding welcome texture to the eerily empty soundscape of the woods. "You said it, not me."

"Sorry to be weird, but how is Tom older than us?"

"He's a 42-year-old 20-year-old. Next year he'll be a 43-year-old 20-year-old."

"I think Sidney might be a 22-year-old 20-year-old."

"Ah," he said. "It begins."

"Mm."

Jay opened his mouth to speak but was interrupted by Sidney screaming, followed closely by a splash and the sound of her cackling into the quiet. She yelled something unintelligible, which was followed by another splash I could only assume was Tom's.

"The call of the void."

Jay laughed. "Oh, yes."

When we reached the bottom of the slope, my arms were wrecked from the brush, scratched in some places, and surely bitten by bugs in others. If we'd gotten eaten alive out here, Tom and Sidney had it worse, having spent at least ten minutes wading half-naked in the murky water. One of their phones had been left face down with the flashlight on, a crude spotlight that gathered an acre's worth of moths.

"Is it cold?" I asked.

"Not really." Sidney held out her arms at her sides and slowly twirled around, the water rippling outward from her waist. She was wearing only a bra and underwear, a uniform I, too, would have to accept if I decided to join her.

"Is it gross?"

"Yeah." Tom, who hadn't spoken since we'd arrived at the base of the cliff, suddenly appeared behind Sidney. He was red-eyed, his hair dripping. Somehow, despite his age and an appearance that would suggest otherwise, he was the absolute picture of a recklessly drunk 20-something, oozing the same state of mind that made frat boys go streaking and steal rival statues. In the span of five seconds I'd managed to reach the liminal space that was knowing exactly what Sidney saw in him and wanting absolutely none of it. As Jay passed me and made his way toward the bank of the creek, it occurred to me that Sidney may have been thinking the same thing about him and me. But it was friendship if anything. In contrast to Tom, Jay was palatable, and he was funny. But he was twice my age—and he looked it. Whatever it was about Tom that got to Sidney made me feel like a child. I still wasn't sold on taking my shirt off.

I looked up from the ground to see Jay staring over his shoulder in my direction. The hand that had just barely slipped under the hem of my dress recoiled, conscious of being watched.

"Sorry," he said, half under his breath.

"It's fine."

Jay turned back around, placing his palm against a tree to support himself as he slipped off his shoes, nestling his socks inside. He was otherwise fully clothed as he waded in, his shirt billowing as it filled up with creek. I slipped out of my dress and rolled it neatly, laying it across the openings of Jay's shoes and feeling briefly weird for doing so.

Sidney was right; the water was far from cold—lukewarm, thick, slimy. Each time I picked up my knees I had to force them through a film and nearly gagged at the resistance.

"This is gross."

Jay laughed. "Just a bit."

"It's clearer once you get away from the edges."

"Uh-huh." I rolled my eyes and followed the line of us that had become to form in front of me, with Sidney leading.

TO SAINTS PETER AND PAUL

The day after I got home from Sidney's, Jay called me. I was sitting in my apartment, eating the last of my Cheerios in my underwear, trying not to think about the fact that it was almost Monday and that I would be expected to show up the following morning to my shitty data-entry job. I almost didn't pick up the phone, but I was curious as to why he would feel the need to call me less than 24 hours after we'd last seen each other. What could be that important that a text message wouldn't suffice? Although, then again, he didn't seem like the texting type.

"Hello?"

"Hey," he said. "Do you want to walk in a cemetery?"

I swallowed my Cheerios. "What?"

"Do you want to go for a walk with me in a cemetery?"

I wasn't sure whether to take him seriously. I half-scoffed/half-laughed, thinking to myself, *Are we in some kind of twee indie movie?* But I didn't want to say that, because I was hurting for friends and there was a nonzero chance he was being genuine. "I have work tomorrow."

"So?" Jay said. "It's only 7:00."

I took another handful of Cheerios out of the box and chewed it loudly, in part so that my obvious being-occupied-with-eating would buy me some time to decide how I wanted to respond.

"Okay," I said eventually. "But we can't be out really late."

"Okay, cool."

"Like, just walking at the cemetery?" I asked, kind of just to hear myself say the words out loud. I couldn't believe what I'd agreed to. I was astral projecting above myself, watching my physical body accept these plans while the rest of me looked on in horror.

"Yeah, we're just walking at the cemetery. I'll pick you up."

"Okay," said the woman standing below me in the kitchen. I was hanging from the ceiling, so I couldn't hear what the man said on the other end of the phone call. Then the woman hung up the phone, put the box of Cheerios away, and got into the shower.

I wasn't thinking about Cody much until I turned the shower on. There was this semester last year where something got mixed up with my student loans and I couldn't put down the deposit for my housing, so Cody let me live with him in his student apartment. It was surprisingly okay, except for some reason he would never let me take a shower by myself. It wasn't that I asked him for permission—it was more that he would just come in there with me. No matter what time I woke up, no matter how tired he was, Cody was called to the shower the way purer and more generous men are called in the service of God. The sounds of the water running were his smelling salts. Grogginess be damned, he would be standing in the bathroom half-hanging out of his underwear in under 45 seconds.

He wouldn't try to have sex with me or anything, either—at least not all the time. He would just stand there, taking up more than his fair share of the shower stream and half-heartedly rubbing his armpits with a vaguely soapy hand. But it was very important, for some reason, that I will be in there with him for this occasion, and that he witnessed all of my own much more thorough shower time activities in their entirety.

Eventually, I got to know his schedule, and I would try to sneak showers in the brief window after I got home from class and before he left work. Sometimes, he would come home early, forcing me to perform the last five minutes of my routine for him. Other times, he would notice my wet hair and be visibly distressed for the next 24 hours. It had occurred to me more than a few times since then that, had we stayed together and eventually shared another apartment, we would have to once again address this situation. In that sense, I had one less thing to worry about.

I didn't know what to wear.

This was my first time attending a walk in a cemetery with a guy in his 40s I met at a party. Not that there was any sort of specific attire recommended for this purpose, but now that I was undressed and freshly showered, I had to go out of my way to make some kind of decision. I found myself saddled with the unique dilemma of dressing for an event that sounded like a bad first date between two goth teenagers while being decidedly non-goth on a not-date with a guy twice my age. I thought about it for a few seconds and then remembered that I didn't even decide to accept Jay's invitation. I was simply floating around near the kitchen ceiling while this dumbass human woman agreed to the plans over the phone. I thought to myself, *Fuck it. If you want to be spontaneous and make weird plans so badly, then you deal with this. This is your burden to bear.*

The woman shivering in a towel a few feet below me didn't know what to wear.

This was her first time attending a walk in a cemetery with a guy in his 40s she met at a party. Not that there was any sort of specific attire recommended for this purpose, but now that she was undressed and freshly showered, she had to go out of her way to make some kind of decision. She'd picked up the phone, she'd agreed to the plans, and now here she was, saddled with the unique dilemma of dressing for an event that sounded like a bad first date between two goth teenagers while being decidedly not-goth on a not-date with a guy twice her age. She combed out her hair before wandering back into the bedroom and throwing on a pair of black tights and black shorts. But that looked like she was trying too hard, or like she was the epitome of some cute 20-something a guy like Jay would snag at a bar or something and then take on adventures. It couldn't be that easy. The woman tried on a few more things. She tried on a dress, but that seemed try-hard also, and there would be mosquitos. Legs need to be covered.

Eventually, she landed on a pair of leggings, a flannel, some nice boots—the things she would have normally worn in the first place. Because that's how these things always go, really: you put on a bunch of different outfits only to realize that anything except your usual costume feels like a costume.

A few minutes later, Jay called to say he was pulling up in front of the building, and my body and I stepped into the car at the same time.

"Hey babe," he said as I shut the door.

"Babe?"

"Oh!" He looked briefly embarrassed. "No. I call everyone that. I call guys that. You can ask Tom."

I laughed. I believed him. It seemed like the easier thing to do, and it's not like he was a total stranger. "No, it's okay. Don't worry about it."

"If it's not okay, I—"

"No, babe is fine."

"Okay."

"Okay." He pulled away from the curb, and I clicked in my seatbelt. "We're going to St. Peter and Paul's. You ever been there?"

"My nana is buried there," I said.

"Ah. My dad is buried there."

"Really? I'm sorry."

"Nah, he was a dick. It's okay." Jay waved his hand dismissively in my direction to signal he hadn't taken offense.

"Well, okay," I said.

"So, you've been?"

"Well, yeah, but not much."

He nodded. "It's really nice, especially at night. You can walk around without anyone bothering you. These little groups of deer come out. Honestly," he said, laughing, "it's probably the largest area of green space in the entire city. The place where we bury our dead."

"That's morbid."

"Yeah, but it is what it is."

"How was your first day back?" I asked, turning the conversation toward the only thing besides dead relatives we were sure to have in common.

"You mean, how am I handling myself after drinking myself stupid and then driving my hungover ass four hours back home the next morning?"

I laughed. "So, you're saying it went well."

"Yeah, it went well. Bought me a couple of bottles of Gatorade on the road. That's all."

"Important question: what flavor?"

"The original, obviously."

"There's an original?"

"The lemon-lime one!" Jay shot back. "That used to be the only flavor. Then they introduced the orange one. Then it was just those two. But you probably don't remember that since you were born in, what, 2005?"

I was laughing more than I thought I would at this kind of joke. "What the fuck? More like 1995, dude."

"Nah, I feel like it was definitely 2005. Do you even remember 9/11?"

"Don't be weird," I said.

Jay wound down almost immediately, taking his eyes off the road briefly to look at me with a serious expression. I'd already gotten the impression from our brief time at Taco House and the preceding few minutes of the car ride that he was the type to listen when he'd gone too far, slowing down at any indication of crossed boundaries. Knowing this helped. "I'm sorry, I don't want to make this weird."

"No, it's alright. Just—"

"Yeah, no, I'm sorry."

Less than a minute later, we arrived at the cemetery. The sun had gone down, so the roads into the grounds were already blocked off. Jay had to park the car at a meter on one of the side streets directly across from the blocked-off main entrance. "So, we're going to have to find a place to squeeze in, since it's technically closed."

I nodded, following Jay's lead as he undid his seatbelt and stepped out of the car.

"I brought red wine and cups. They're in the trunk if you want them." Jay gestured toward the trunk before leaning back into the car and shuffling around for something in the glove compartment.

I opened the trunk and pulled out a reusable grocery bag with a package of Solo cups and what looked like an unopened bottle. I looked around to see if anyone else was standing nearby and gently slid the bottle out of the bag. It was some kind of red blend with an outline of a howling wolf on the label. I hadn't had this specific variety before, but as a frequent patron of the lower shelves in the liquor store, I recognized it as one of the cheaper kinds. "Nice," I said, just to have something to say.

"Hey, there's some green here too, if you want it," Jay said a little too loudly, quickly flashing me a glimpse of some pre-rolled joints in a Ziploc bag.

"Sure," I said.

"Bring them?"

"Yeah, bring them."

Jay slid the bag into his pocket. He closed the car door and relieved me of the grocery bag. We crossed the street, and he began walking ahead of me around the side of the cemetery grounds.

"We don't have to, like, climb a fence or something?"

"No, we shouldn't have to." We were on a narrow, bumpy, asphalt path beside the cemetery itself, nestled between the fence and a line of trees. "There's usually one or two of these left open."

I didn't understand what he meant, but we kept walking.

After a while, I said, "I don't know why they even have to keep these places so secure. It's a cemetery. Do they think people are going to, like, unbury the bodies? I don't get it."

"Maybe they don't want degenerates sneaking in here to drink after hours." Jay didn't turn around to look at me but held the bag up as a gesture.

"Fair enough."

After another minute, we wound up at a slightly-open unlocked gate connecting the asphalt strip we'd been walking on to one of the cemetery's footpaths. Jay reached behind him and handed off the bag before leaning into the gate to push it the rest of the way open. Black paint flaked off of the metal as it crossed the ground with an unnerving screech.

Jay turned around with this tongue-in-cheek serial killer smile. "Creepy, isn't it?"

"Yeah," I said, and we went in.

"I wanna get kind of far away from the edges," Jay said. "I don't think anyone is really going to see us or care, but, you know, just in case."

I nodded, once again letting Jay lead. We followed the footpath the entire way, choosing the turns and tributaries that would lead us deeper into the labyrinth. There were small patches of trees breaking up the monotony of the gravestones, a vague sense that the burial plots were organized in some intentional way, but I didn't know much about cemeteries, having deliberately not spent much time in them. It didn't take long for me to feel certain that, should Jay leave me there alone for any reason, I wouldn't be able to find my way out. Not that it was going to come to that, although there was no discounting the possibility.

We finally stopped by a mausoleum and sat down, leaning against the wall. Jay placed the bag with the wine and cups between us. My stomach dropped, partially due to the nature of the setting and partially due to some residue left over from college years and being underage, not wanting to get caught with any sort of alcohol under any circumstances. It occurred to me that, should anyone catch us drinking here late at night, the most that would happen was that we would get kicked out or possibly fined. Maybe there was some slight chance we could be pinned for some other minor crime, like public intoxication, But in any case, judging by Jay's seemingly deliberate choice of a drinking spot and the confidence with which he was traversing the cemetery at this hour, walking and drinking with me was far from his first rodeo. He knew what we could get away with, and we would be just fine.

Jay pulled the joints out of his pocket. "Weed first? Wine first?" he asked.

"Weed first," I said. It seemed better to get the more incriminating thing out of the way, and as a bonus, it would help with my anxiety.

"As you wish."

There was this thing about Jay that I had noticed glimpses of but until this moment couldn't entirely pin down. He was dorky. But not in the classical sense. Not, like, fedoras and *The Hobbit* or something. It was the way he spoke, and it was only sometimes—that little "as you wish," these little gestures. I hadn't done this consciously, but I'd begun to perceive it as some sort of holdover from being younger and maybe not as popular and maybe not as smooth with women. For the most part, he could get by okay nowadays, say all of the normal, well-adjusted adult things. But then once in a while, some quaint little anachronism would slip past the fail-safes and come trickling out, surprising both of us. I found it endearing, but I knew better than to draw too much attention.

He handed me one of the joints and a lighter and began opening the wine bottle, leaving me to get the joint started. Sitting there with the joint in my one hand and a lighter in the other—this sort of some-assembly-required smoking experience—I realized once again that I'd always had someone to do this sort of thing for me: Sidney, Cody, one of his friends. I stuck what I hoped was the right end of the joint between my lips, trying to recall an instance where I'd done a drug someone hadn't simply handed to me, hadn't already gotten started.

Luckily for me, Jay turned around at this exact moment and held out his hand. "You need a light?"

I nodded, placing the lighter in his open palm. I leaned in, stopping an inch or two from where he had positioned it. I was still a good foot or so from Jay's face, but I could see him in drastically more detail than I'd had at any point this evening, or even at Taco House. He looked older, but not as much older as I was expecting him to look. His eyes were still kind, still wet, still had that thing in them that I didn't see in most of my professors, other authority figures, my parents when they were this same age. He smiled, lighting the end of the joint, and the skin around his lips stretched and folded into warm, well-worn valleys.

I inhaled, pulled the joint out of my mouth, inhaled a little extra, exhaled. This part I knew.

"Alright, here we go," Jay said, rubbing his hands together.

I took another hit and then handed it to him, peered around his body to check the status of the wine and cups while trying not to make it obvious.

He finished his hit, coughed slightly. "Easy, wino," he teased. "We'll toast in just a moment." I smiled and sat back against the wall.

"Hey," Jay said after a while, "Maybe once we finish up here, we could visit your grandma."

"Huh?"

"Saint Peter and Paul's," he said as he gestured around. "You said your grandma was buried here or something?"'

"Oh," I said. "Yeah, but I don't know where."

"You don't know where your grandma is buried?"

I shrugged.

"Well, alright."

Jay and I continued working on the joint, passing it back and forth at more-or-less equal intervals. After a few volleys, he declared he didn't want or need to smoke anymore, and that I could finish it off if I so desired. I declined if only from the shock at someone I was spending time with not wanting to smoke every last bit of weed available to them. Among my other friends or even Cody's friends, this was just not something that happened. It was simply never done.

"Had a weird day yesterday," Jay said, having done what was necessary to curtail the joint and get us started on the wine.

"Oh yeah?"

"Yeah, and I mean after the long hungover drive. I took a nap, then met up with my friend Lori; she was in town for this reading thing, like a charity event." I nodded along as he spoke. "We ended up driving around after and just having this long talk about what it's like now, to be this age and to live like this." He gestured around him at the Solo cups, the wine, the cemetery grounds around us—all of these things making his point in more of a literal way than he probably intended.

"How do you mean?" I asked, just to move things along.

"You know, at some point, you realize that all of the normal stuff—the job, house, kids—none of that stuff is working. And some people just do those things anyway. They have this thing that life is supposed to be hard, and it helps them to just move forward with all of it. That's my brother, you know. He just has this thing where he needs to be responsible, and that's fine. But some people just decide to go this other way, try to make something else out of it."

"Right."

"And I've gotten very lucky. You know? I make exactly as much as I need, I get paid under the table, cheap rent. And I know if there was ever a point where times got hard, there are people I could go to, and they'd set me up. They'd say, 'Oh, I know a guy who needs somebody to do this thing or that thing.' There's not much I have to worry about in that sense. And if you're lucky and you put in the time and effort, you can sort of carve out this thing that you want, without having to do any of those other things. And you can get to a point where things are simple." He was saying "things" a lot, but none of it was unclear.

I shrugged. "That sounds nice to me."

"Right," Jay said. "But when you do this, when you decide to live this way, you end up giving up a lot of things. Obviously, there are sacrifices. And then you get a point where you're in your 40s—Lori and I are both in our 40s—and there isn't a blueprint for this when you haven't done the house, kids, career, those things. Where do you go, you know?"

He was slurring a bit, and not entirely due to intoxication, speaking with the same slow, smoky cadence I'd heard him use the night we were drinking together at Taco House. His eyes were fixed elsewhere, on some random grave a few hundred feet away. He was talking to me, but I could tell that the pretense of a conversation with me was just a utilitarian construct at this point. I could nod and express understanding, and it would be helpful to do so, but the ultimate function of this conversation was for Jay to express something that needed to be expressed, likely to anyone at all, likely sooner rather than later. That it was me on this night in this cemetery was just a coincidence. But it was hard to feel bothered in the slightest, as every word he'd spoken up to this point had conveyed just how vital it was that this angst is released.

"I'm 45. I'm up there, you know? Not too up there, but up there. Eventually, something is going to happen to me. I have no insurance. No kids to take care of me. The network that has helped to hold me up, now they're getting up there, too. They're dead, some of them. And there's no plan for what to do when we start really needing to hold each other. Most of us aren't going to be able to do it."

I nodded uselessly.

"What I'm saying is, there's an expiration date on this. And it feels soon. And nobody knows the answer. Lori and I were both in the same spot on this. Last night we didn't get any closer to figuring out what's next."

"Right, yeah," I said.

"I just hope it's something."

"It will be," I said. "It has to be something." My words felt hollow and stupid. I meant them, but only as much as I could mean them as a 22-year-old, and one who had only started down the path of deciding how much normalness I wanted or could even handle.

Jay sighed. "I fuckin' hope so." Then, without so much as a brief pause, he picked up one of the Solo cups and handed it to me. Like he hadn't just unloaded the mother of all burdens. Like there was somehow nothing left to solve or discuss. "To Saints Peter and Paul," he said, holding up his cup and gently tapping it against mine.

We both took long sips, essentially chugging our entire cups at once. By the time I set my cup down on the ground beside me, I was already buzzing. I stared out into the array of trees and graves, hearing the distant-sounding tap of Jay's empty cup touching down next to mine.

"Hey," Jay said, stretching his pointed finger out in front of me. "If you look really close that way, you can see a couple of deer. You see 'em?"

THE DALMATIAN

After the cemetery, Jay and I didn't hang out again for the rest of the week, but we Facebook messaged. My job required roughly three hours of actually focused participation per eight-hour workday, so I had ample time to talk and goof off at my desk. Jay—I wasn't sure what he did, exactly. Odd jobs, some kind of physical labor from Craigslist, only a few hours a day, only a few days a week. He messaged me on the off-days and the off-hours. They weren't particularly deep or substantial conversations, just observations about our days, maybe a music recommendation. On Thursday, he was doing demolition in an abandoned house and sent me a picture of a tiny dog figurine he'd found sitting against the wall in a decrepit bathroom. It was a dalmatian, or what a dalmatian would look like rendered by someone who had received the description of a dalmatian via single, frantic radio transmission. The head was comically small, the eyes lopsided and seemingly staring in two different directions, and it was hollow inside, with an ear missing. This dalmatian had seen some shit.

I want it, I said.

Yeah? I can bring it, Jay messaged back.

Yeah, I said, *bring it*.

And that's how I made plans for Jay to pick me up from work the following day.

The plans were vague. Go to the park, maybe? Smoke, maybe? It seemed odd, but we had somehow already reached the point in our friendship where it didn't matter exactly what we were doing so long as we were in each other's company.

Sidney and I met up for dinner on Thursday night, and when I told her about Jay and the dalmatian and our plans for Friday, she thought it was weird.

"I'm still surprised you went to the cemetery with him," she said.

"Well, it's not like he was a complete stranger," I reasoned. "I wasn't totally irresponsible."

Sidney shook her head and sipped her beer slowly. "Yeah," she said, still swallowing, "but what good would that do if he chopped you into little pieces?"

"He was fine at Taco House!"

Sidney raised her eyebrows. "We were all wasted at Taco House."

You invited him, I wanted to say, but I didn't. I picked up my beer and took a sip, staring into it as I did. When I set my glass down, I said, "Well, either way, it worked out," and Sidney shrugged.

"So, was it, like, a date?"

"No? I don't know? I feel like I would know if it was a date." This was debatable, as I'd more or less only dated Cody, and for our first date we'd gone to Chipotle and eaten the food in his car before leaving to get drunk together at his friends' apartment, but Sidney didn't need to know this.

"But you can't say for sure that it wasn't."

"No."

"And he's—?"

"45," I sighed.

"Hmm." She pouted in this thoughtful way as if mulling the whole thing over. "Okay."

"What?!"

"Nothing," she said, hiding this tiny smile behind her half-empty beer glass. "Just okay." We were both quiet for a few minutes, and then she asked, "Hey, what's a pretzel roll?"

We were eating at this kind of gimmicky burger restaurant near my apartment. The whole premise of the place was that, instead of putting in a normal burger order and choosing from a predefined list of menu items, you used these little check sheets to design your own burger. You could get a normal beef hamburger on a sesame seed bun with lettuce and ketchup, or you could get a portobello mushroom on a ciabatta roll with jalapeño peppers and peanut butter. It was a bastion of trendy, hipster gluttony while also very clearly illustrating the pitfalls of letting people make their own burger decisions, namely the fact that laypeople have shitty burger instincts. It was common to find that the burger you'd designed, one which had seemed like such an obvious win, in theory, was utter trash in practice and all over the map flavor-wise. The best approach was to try and recreate something you remembered eating elsewhere, but it was hard not to deviate wildly when confronted with so many options.

I looked up from my order sheet where I had begun my futile attempt to design a passable burger with both avocado and blue cheese on it. "I think it's like a normal burger bun but it's, like, a pretzel on the outside? I only ever get the Hawaiian roll. It's sweet and lighter, kind of. It's pretty good."

"I'm just going to get a normal bun," Sidney said.

The waitress came around, and we sent in our burger orders by handing her the sheets we'd filled out. When she was gone, I pulled out my phone and showed Sidney the photo of the dalmatian.

"What are you going to do with it?"

"I don't know, put it in my apartment. Put it by the window."

"You should put it outside next to your door. Ward off intruders."

"Guard Dog."

"Guard Dog!" We both laughed a little. "I mean, I wouldn't come in if I saw that."

"Someone would probably steal it, though. Someone keeps stealing my packages. Did I tell you about that?"

"No. What?"

"Yeah," I said, "Somebody keeps stealing my Amazon packages while I'm at work. Like, it'll say they're delivered, but then they won't be there and they'll never show up. So, I'm guessing someone keeps taking them."

"Holy shit," said Sidney, "What kind of stuff? Like, what do they steal?"

"The latest thing they stole was one of those Swiffer sweeper things. And then this one time they stole a big package that had a few different things in it. A vibrator."

She sat back, laughing.

"Yeah. Hope they're enjoying it, I guess," I said.

"No doubt."

We continued working on our drinks, neither of us saying much. Sidney was typing something on her phone, so I pulled mine out and scrolled through different apps, looking for something to look at it. A guy I'd had a class with in college had shared an article about Chris Cornell from Soundgarden and his recent death.

I looked up from my phone. "Have you heard anything from Cody lately?"

Sidney, still engrossed in whatever was happening on her screen, shook her head at me. "I mean, we didn't really talk much as it is. We only knew each other –"

"Through me, yeah." My face was hot. I reached for my drink just to have another thing to do with my hands, to somehow stave off the mounting feeling that I'd ripped something open by asking.

"Why?"

"I don't know. Chris Cornell died."

Sidney looked up from her phone, her eyebrows cinched toward the center of her forehead. "He told me he called you that day and you hung up on him."

"I thought you said you hadn't really talked to him."

"I didn't. Ant told me."

Ant was Sidney's boyfriend. They'd been together on and off for the better part of three years but never put a label on it. They'd been on vacations together, met each other's parents. I didn't know anyone who knew them and didn't think of them as a unit. Ant and Sidney. *Oh, are Ant and Sidney going to be there?* But something about this troubled Ant for reasons that seemed hidden even from him. Every few months, Sidney would make the case for an Official Relationship, and Ant would recoil and break up with her for a few weeks. They would each see other people, and then Ant would get jealous that Sidney was seeing someone who wasn't him, and they would get back together again. Once, in the midst of all of this drama, Ant had ended up at a house show where Cody was also present. They'd bonded over a mutual love of vinyl records, thus completing the circle and ensuring that none of us would ever be spared an update on each other's business.

"I always forget they talk now," I said.

"I think it's good. Cody helps keep him in line. Speaking of which," Sidney locked her phone and placed it on the edge of the table near the wall. "So, Ant went out last night, and usually when he goes out—I don't know what he does—but he starts getting all prickly. Like he's feeling suffocated or something. But last night, he went out with Cody."

"Oh yeah?"

"Yeah, and he asked to *swing by* on his way back, and we watched a movie together with popcorn. And he's taking me out for Indian after work tomorrow night."

"Two nights in a row?" I asked with genuine surprise.

"Yeah, like, that never happens. That's what I'm saying. Cody is a good influence on him."

"I'm glad for you," I said.

"What even went down between you guys anyway?"

I sighed. This was the exact reason I'd been hesitating to bring Cody up at all, not just with Sidney but with anyone. Having coached other friends of mine through serious breakups, I knew that any reason I gave for leaving would seem inconsequential. Nobody wants to hear about long-term relationships falling apart. It makes the prospect of lasting love seem all the more impossible, erodes some precious institution that you, as the participant in a long-term relationship, have been involuntarily tasked with upholding for any nearby witnesses. Sidney was damn near the only friend I had who wasn't also close to Cody. I knew she wouldn't like this regardless.

"I guess I was bored," I said. "Not like we didn't do anything fun together. We did stuff. He just started to seem like he was...done."

"Done, like, with you?"

"Like, done. Like complete. A fully complete person. I would get in his car and he would be listening to the same two albums. Just the same two albums he was really into when we first met. Like, I guess that's it, that's just music now? I don't know."

"Nothing wrong with a preference," Sidney said.

"And he would keep telling me the same stories about them like it was the first time I'd ever gotten into his car and he was listening to those albums. And I would have to be like, 'Oh yeah, that's really cool,' like I wasn't bored out of my mind about it. And he didn't want to move out of his parents' house. He would be like, 'Oh, but then we wouldn't have the big TV'—because his parents have this huge TV in the basement that we always watched movies on. And he always wanted to have sex the same way every time. Like, every time I would be on top."

"Hey. Nothing wrong with a preference," she said again, laughing this time.

"No, but it wasn't a preference. It was every single time! I would always have to be on top of him. We would get started, and he would just wait for me to do it. And I'd have to say the same sort of things. He wouldn't even talk or make any noise or anything like he was enjoying it. Then afterward I would be like, 'That was fun," and he would nod or something. It was stupid."

Sidney took a large swig of her beer, belching softly as the glass hit the table.

"I don't know, he was just too content with everything. He believed too much in everything he said. It freaked me out. How do you spend your entire life with someone who doesn't think they're ever going to learn anything else? One time he said that he couldn't think of any time in high school where he'd done anything embarrassing. A single embarrassing thing. From high school. That's so bad!"

"I don't know," Sidney said. "Kind of wish Ant would be that sure about something. Literally anything. Last year on Valentine's Day he kept me on edge all day because he wasn't sure if agreeing to go to dinner with me was too much. And I was just sitting there, like, 'Obviously you're going to decide to come get me, so can you just do it? Stop worrying so much about what everything Means,' you know?"

"Yeah."

"What did he even make you say?"

"What?"

"What did he make you say? Like, in bed?"

I looked down, shaking my head. "Just like, I don't know, 'You have such a fat cock,' or whatever. Which was fine, but I just hated how it was always the same thing. It was always 'fat cock.' It was such a specific, weird thing, and it felt weird to say it."

"Yeah," Sidney mumbled, gesturing next to us with her eyes.

I looked over and realized the server had been standing beside our table, holding our burgers. I sat back, letting him place his plate in front of me with the stony detachment of someone desperate to leave their own body and/or be transfigured into a lamp.

"Thank you," I said.

GUARD DOG

The next day, Jay picked me up after work. He didn't know which building I was in and ended up parking a few blocks away on a side street. When I opened the passenger-side door, the dalmatian was positioned in the seat with the seatbelt fastened over it, nearly covering its whole body.

"Aww, he was safe," I said, picking up the dalmatian and climbing inside.

I felt Jay smiling at me. "There are laws about these things," he said matter-of-factly.

"Yeah. Imagine if you got pulled over."

Jay pulled away from the curb. Once he could afford to pay less attention to the road, he turned to look at me. "You look nice," he said.

"Thanks." I pushed down a grin and kept my attention on the dalmatian, staring intently at its misaligned eyes. I figured it wasn't too weird of a compliment. I was wearing my work clothes, which skewed a little nicer than anything I would have worn to the cemetery or Taco House. "Business casual," I said in a sort of low, mocking voice.

"My condolences."

I shrugged. "It's fine. Makes me feel like I'm playing adult for a few hours a day."

Jay slowed down the car as we approached the red light at the end of the next block. "Everybody's playing adult," he said.

"You're right." He was, but it was weird to say it.

The light had turned green, and we'd turned onto one of the city's wider, busier streets lined with all of these financial buildings. I liked watching people pour out of them—how they wore the same things, took all of these specific actions—as if in agreement with one of a small handful of preselected scripts for their behavior. I liked all of this, in the same way, I liked walking into the office for my data entry job. I liked seeing everyone else in their business casual. I liked how tired people looked, how it validated, and contextualized my tiredness. I liked the mornings where I would encounter someone else in the elevator, and we would exchange a look of severe exhaustion, as if mutually validating our personhood, acknowledging the depressing reality of having to spend half of our waking hours wearing business casual and sitting in a cold office. In those moments, I understood our culture's obsession with Honest Work, with being one of the Workers. You weren't happy 80% of the time, but you knew you were part of something; it was the unhappiness that connected you to others.

As we drove, I thought about what Jay had said the other night at the cemetery about the cost of falling out of all of this. He seemed to think there was something to be gained in risking alienation, but when I thought about how many times my day was improved just by sharing glances with someone who looked just as worn-out as I did, it seemed hard to believe.

"So, I thought we could eat something," Jay said after a few moments. "Then go for a drive. Or there's the park if you'd rather."

"Alright."

"There's wine in the back, too. For later." He cleared his throat. "If you so desire."

I nodded to indicate that I so desired.

We decided on Mexican. Jay said there was a little hole-in-the-wall place about twenty minutes outside the city. It was a little out of the way, but it had some of the best Mexican he'd ever had, and it was worth the trip as long as I wasn't overly hungry. I was starved, but I agreed. Jay had talked the place up, and I wasn't in any particular rush to get home.

We spent most of the drive not talking, with Jay interrupting every so often to tell an anecdote about some town or building we were passing, or to comment on the music. When he was younger, he rented a shitty apartment a few blocks from here. This building used to be a pub or a laundromat. When this album was written, the frontman thought he was terminally ill and was trying to cope with his impending death. Here was where his stepdad used to pick up food on the way home from his job at the factory, back when there still were jobs and factories. There's a great essay about this song written by Lester Bangs.

I listened to everything Jay said, but I couldn't look at him. After what he'd said at the red light, there was some kind of blockage. Like his eyes were too much, or like he was too old for them to be what they were—still, at 45, so big and wet, like fruits that had been frozen and preserved. I would try to steal a glance and feel suddenly bloated. I kept my head turned toward the window, holding the dalmatian in one of my fists and rubbing its face with my thumb to scan its features.

Eventually, we pulled up to the restaurant. Jay had said it was a hole-in-the-wall joint, and he hadn't been kidding. It looked more like an oversized shed than an eating establishment: the sign on the front worn to the point of unreadability and only one other car parked in the small gravel lot. "This is us," Jay said. We got out of the car, and I placed the dalmatian on the dashboard. As we headed inside, I looked over my shoulder and saw it staring at me through the windshield, its mismatched eyes holding in them more intent than any object had the right to.

"Should I have cracked the window for him?" Jay had noticed me looking back at his car and stopped a few feet ahead of me, just short of the door of the restaurant. When I turned to look at him, he had this goofy grin on his face, like he was building up to a specific punchline.

"Nah," I said. "For some reason, I feel like he's smart enough to do it himself if he needs to."

"He's the brains of this operation."

"Guard dog," I said.

Jay gave a nod that felt official. "Guard dog."

He led us to a table in the back without waiting to be seated. A few minutes later an older woman who I assumed for some reason was the owner walked over, and we each ordered something off of the one-page laminated menu that had been sitting in the center of the table.

When the woman walked away, he said, "So, you see how run-down it is in here?"

I cringed. He was speaking quietly, but the place was practically empty, and I was sure the owner could hear us. "Yeah."

"That's how you can tell the food is good. The worse the place looks, the better the food is."

"What if it's a new place?"

"Then it's a new place." Jay didn't seem interested in having his theory challenged. He reached over and lifted the menu from the table beside us. "Same with the menus," he said. "The more options you have, the worse the food is. You want to go to a place that sells, like, ten things."

"Ten things," I repeated. "Last night I went to this place that had so many options you had to custom order your burger. Like, dozens of toppings. You had to write it down separately."

"Dozens of toppings." Jay leaned forward, looking intrigued. "And was it good?"

"Yeah."

"Well, still," he said. "Small menu; it's just one burger you customize in different ways. My theory still holds up."

"But it was also a new place," I said.

"So what?"

"So, it was a new place!"

Jay rolled his eyes, placing the menu back on the other table as he lifted himself out of his chair. "I'm gonna go to the bathroom. Hold down the fort. Get me a drink if she comes back."

I nodded, and before I could ask Jay what kind of drink he wanted, he disappeared down the narrow hallway in the back corner of the restaurant.

I sat back in my chair. With Jay gone and the owner busy in the back, I was currently the only person in the room. My solitude made the place feel even less like a restaurant. I was starting to have less-than-ideal thoughts. That is, I was starting to see this entire outing from a third-person point of view. I was a 22-year-old girl-woman, sitting in a run-down Mexican restaurant an absurd distance from home, on a Friday night, still dressed in my Business Casual, waiting for the 45-year-old guy I was hanging out with to get out of the bathroom. This guy made these plans with me under the pretense of giving me a little ceramic dalmatian. And after this was over, we were going to go to a park and drink wine together. I began to wonder if Jay had considered these things if he was at all concerned about how weird it was. It occurred to me that maybe this was the reason he'd chosen to take me someplace so far away, someplace where there would be few other patrons to judge us, someplace nobody he knew would be likely to show up and see him with basically a child.

The waitress came back over to our table to check on us, and I ordered jalapeno margaritas for both myself and Jay. Besides red wine, I had no idea what Jay's taste in alcohol entailed. I was banking on the possibility that he would at least find my choice of drink adventurous or decidedly Not Lame, even if he didn't like it. He arrived back at the table right after I decided on our drinks, passing the owner on his way back to his seat. I did my best to snap back into shape, giving the impression that everything was exactly as he'd left it and nothing new had crossed my mind, not a hair out of place.

"I got us margaritas," I said.

"That's fine."

We sat quietly for a few minutes as Jay pulled out his phone and began scrolling absentmindedly. I found myself looking over my shoulder every few seconds to glance at the door, both wanting someone new to show up and hoping they wouldn't.

"So, you come here—a lot?" I asked, narrowly avoiding The Line.

"As much as I can, I guess." Jay finished up whatever he'd been doing on his phone and returned his attention to me. "I mean, for how far it is. But yeah, I like it here. Why do you ask?"

"It's just a little far, that's all," I lied.

"Ah," he said, nodding in a way that suggested he didn't completely believe me but was content to let it go. "Yeah. It's worth it. Plus, I like to take people here."

Only the other 22-year-olds, though, I thought to myself. Another spiral of less-than-ideal thoughts. *The ones your friends can't see you with.*

"Cool," I said. I was afraid of what else I would end up saying if I continued, so I looked over my shoulder again, watching no one come through the door.

"Tom and I come here a lot. I like the quiet."

Tom, the other old guy from Taco House, one of Jay's friends and decidedly not a 22-year-old. Good. This was good. I turned my focus back to the conversation, looking, I'm sure, suddenly relaxed. "Yeah, it's a way different vibe than just being downtown or something," I said uselessly.

"Yeah, the only thing is you can't customize your burger."

"I'll survive!" I clutched my hand to my chest in an act of performative resilience.

"Will you?"

Both of us laughed. Shortly after, the waitress brought over our drinks. Jay picked up his glass, took a small sip, winced, and said, "Spicy."

"Yeah, it's jalapeño," I said.

"Yeah." He took another sip without wincing, this time having prepared for it. "So," he said, "are we going to talk about him?"

"Huh?"

"Corey, or whatever."

"Cody." I picked up my margarita and poured a larger-than-average swig down my throat. "I don't really have anything to say. I don't know. Whatever thing you're trying to do..."

"I'm not trying to do a thing," Jay said, and then drank, his wet eyes insistent in their goofiness as he looked down his nose at me over the glass.

"I already told you, anyway," I said. "I broke up with him. We haven't talked. I think this weekend he's supposed to come over. Get a box of his stuff."

Jay swallowed, nodded, set down his drink with a pointed *mm*. "The Exit Interview."

Against my wishes, I smiled. "Yeah, I guess."

"I never liked those. It should just be that you ship everything."

"I thought about it. But he insisted on coming."

"Of course he did. He's gonna try to change your mind, or negotiate. That's the Exit Interview." He worked on his drink. "He'll ask you what went wrong and whatever you say he'll try to solve it somehow. You're better off just not telling him anything."

"So, should I tell him not to come?"

"No," Jay said. "Now he's just going to come anyway. Just don't let him stay too long. It has to be clean. Open the door, give him the stuff, he leaves."

"What if he doesn't want to leave?" I asked.

"Put me on standby," he replied quickly. As if by instinct, the characteristic flicker of mischief in his eyes compensating for any weird paternal vibes.

For the rest of the meal, I didn't look over my shoulder once.

After dinner, when Jay and I got back to the car, I took the dalmatian off of the dashboard and held it up in the quickly-waning sunlight. There was a jagged half-circle of white residue on the flared bottom, where the dog's ass and all four of its paws converged into one flat, featureless plane where a small label had at some point been poorly removed. Up until now, I'd been conceiving of the dalmatian as this random, single occurrence: a unique object that had just happened to end up in a place where Jay had been at the time he'd been there, either by chance or as part of some carefully-delineated series of cosmic events. But this white residue revealed the potential existence of additional dalmatians, sitting side-by-side on a shelf in some novelty store from which this particular dalmatian was selected and removed from circulation a month or year or decade ago—there was no way to know how long it had been since this particular dog was taken off the grid. There was at least some chance this dalmatian was even older than I was. It boasted some long and storied past whose details were virtually unknowable and would forever be hidden from us.

"Are we going to the park?" Jay said.

"Yeah," I said. I climbed into the car and placed the dalmatian in my lap, holding it steady with one hand.

Jay started the car, and we rolled out of the gravel lot, back toward civilization. He cranked the air and futzed with the stereo for a few minutes until a run of plucked notes came wavering out into the stale, still-hot air. "Kevin Morby's 'Harlem River,'" he said, gesturing toward the stereo.

I nodded, making no indication as to whether or not I already knew this information. It didn't feel especially important. There was no pressure to assert my knowledge of music or push back against what may have been some attempt on his part to do the same. We were dealing, as we'd always been, in moments: an egoless pursuit to set the perfect thing afloat above the rush of the overtaxed AC. And tonight Kevin Morby was almost too on-the-nose, crooning *Harlem River, talk to me / Where we headed now?* as Jay's car rumbled off onto some side road, diverting from the route we'd taken to get there.

I was about to ask where we were going when he gestured toward his glove box, asking me to open it. When he did, he pulled out a joint, lit it, and tossed the lighter into the center console in one fluid motion. He took a short puff before erupting into a fit of dry coughs.

As he passed the joint to me, he nodded at the windshield and said, "Gotta go scenic route if you wanna do this."

I took a hit, making an attempt at a steady exhale before exploding into a coughing fit of my own and, in turn, destroying any remaining potential to seem graceful or well-versed.

Jay wove down a series of mostly-deserted roads, keeping us parallel to the highway as we smoked. We were silent, our highs mounting as the song played. *I climbed a cloud / And now I stole the moon / Harlem River / All because of you.* When we finished, he tossed the roach out the window and directed us back onto I-79. The sun had begun to go down, and the road looked foreign now in the bluish light.

After a couple of minutes, I said, "Thanks for taking me."

Jay grinned and laughed quietly to himself. "The pleasure is mine."

"What?"

He kept his eyes focused on the road, shaking his head slightly. "It's a Friday night and you could be out with anybody, and you're out in the middle of nowhere with some old dude."

"I don't have anybody else to hang out with."

I looked at Jay and winced. Before the sentence had completely exited my mouth, I'd already begun mapping out potential means of damage control. I hadn't intended it as an insult, or even a joke; I was only telling the truth, but for Jay to somehow pick up on this obscure intention seemed unlikely. But he didn't seem taken aback, even jokingly so.

Instead, he asked, "Yeah, what's up with that?"

It was the sort of question you wouldn't ask rhetorically, at least the way Jay had. Nobody had asked this sort of thing of me and meant it, and I found myself at a loss. "I don't know," I said. Then, before it could be caught or edited, another sentence spilled out of my mouth. "I don't like anyone right now."

"Why don't you like anyone right now?"

Kevin Morby had stopped singing, and we'd moved onto the next thing in Jay's playlist. Something artsy sounding, something 80s; I didn't know it and it didn't matter.

"Something broke," I said. "I just stopped."

Jay grunted. "Well, you like me."

"Yeah," I said.

"Why?"

"Do you not believe me?" I turned my focus toward Jay and away from the window I'd been staring out of. Maybe it was the change in context or lighting, but his face suddenly looked unreadable and oddly harsh.

"I believe you," he said. "I just thought maybe it would help you if you could figure out why."

"Ah."

I stopped to think, and the song expanded to fill the space of Jay's car, lush and foreboding. *Penthouse perfection / But what goes on? / What to do there?* As the verse tore on, we took small, inconspicuous breaths, as if we might get away with something. When it ended, Jay said, "Roxy Music."

"Oh," I said.

Jay continued. "This song's about a blow-up doll."

"Really?"

"That's what they say."

"The band?"

"No. Just, like, people."

We listened for a few more seconds, and then I said, "I don't know why. It might just be that you're new."

"New?"

I sighed "To me. Like—"

"Like a sweater," he interrupted. "New to you."

I nodded, relieved. "Yeah." I looked out the window awhile and then asked, "Are you okay with that?"

"Yeah."

We were silent for the next leg of the trip. Night had descended on the crowding highway and I stared out, thinking nothing. I filtered all my awareness to the dalmatian, running my thumb back and forth along its scarred bottom. It was the closest I'd ever been to complete blankness, to zero thoughts. Then, in what felt like an instant, we were nearing the city again, and Jay was veering off toward an exit that looked familiar.

By the time we got to the park, the sky was black. Jay's car was parked at the top of a slope, his front bumper inches from a wooden guard rail. It wasn't so much the park as it was a winding road that would take you into and out of it, but it was no disappointment. You could see the whole city from here, geometric and twinkling at the bottom of a bowl. I stepped out of the car, leaving the dalmatian in my seat. Jay was already behind me, rifling around in the trunk for wine and cups. The fact that in the past seven days I had gone on two separate outings with Jay specifically to sit in the dark and drink wine out of cups was both surprising and not. He handed me a plastic bag holding a stack of cups, took the wine himself, and led me down the road towards a bench. We sat down, poured the wine, passed the cups, following the steps in this new routine we'd already nailed.

"Good?" he said.

"Good."

We both took large swigs of the wine.

"I like it up here," Jay said. "Stays pretty quiet."

Sometimes you have these moments that feel wistful before they've even had a chance to play out in full like it's all written with this air of retrospection. I'd been feeling it the entire night with Jay, but especially now. Sitting beside him, looking down at the city, there was this sense of things being burned in, of watching in real-time the inscription of nostalgia. It sounds holy when described this way, and it is, but the holiness comes with its own pressure. You start to behave in weird ways when you know your conversation has already made the highlight reel.

"I have a question," I said.

"Shoot."

"Is this weird?"

"Huh?"

"I don't know. I don't know if you just see me as a kid or something."

Jay's face was difficult to see in the dark. I could hear him breathing into his cup for a moment, then a loud gulp, a swish as it went down. "I don't get it. What do you want to know?" he asked, sounding more concerned or confused than impatient. But the moment had already passed, and I was now acutely aware of how disconnected my thoughts were beginning to sound.

"I don't know. Don't worry about it. I'm just throwing things at the wall."

"Ah." Jay and I drank in silence for a while, and then he said, "So, Exit Interview tomorrow."

I inhaled sharply as I nodded. "Not necessarily tomorrow."

"Well, probably."

"Yeah, probably," I said.

"Why did you do it anyway?"

"Like, break up with him?"

"Yeah."

"I don't know." I'd already finished my wine but was sucking absently on the lip of the cup, creating these loud, sloppy echoes. "I just wasn't happy."

"That's diplomatic," Jay said.

"Okay, so?"

"So, he's not going to believe that."

"There's not some list, though," I said. "Of, like, reasons."

"Well, it's what you said before, right?" The low visibility and lack of eye contact made Jay's voice smooth and prophetic. "Something broke; you don't like anyone."

"That's not the same thing," I said. "Or it was more that he was always so serious. He was in charge of every single thing, and he wasn't even good at it."

Jay coughed on his wine.

"No, I mean it!" I exclaimed, my buzzed laughter bubbling up. "Like, he was *strict*. I would post something on Facebook that he didn't agree with, and he would call me later like, 'Hey, I feel that post reflects badly on me.' Like he was my boss."

"Like, you would make posts about him?"

"No, just about other things," I said. "Which is even stupider. Like politics or something. And he would say it makes him look bad how outspoken I am about certain things. And we would have this big argument where I would be like, 'Well, it's my post, it has nothing to do with you,' and he would be like, 'Well, my family can see your posts,' and then I would just end up deleting it because it was too much work to explain why it shouldn't matter what I'm posting about on Facebook. And it would be stuff he agreed with. He just didn't like how vocal I was about things, I guess."

I was on a tear, forgoing all pre-screening of my speech. I'd had a lot to smoke and drink—that department of my mind was gravely understaffed. The girl continued to talk to the man on the bench, and I watched, dangling from the guard rail, gripping hard lest I be sucked away into the swirling blackness at the foot of the slope.

"And it didn't even have to be, like, a hot-button issue. One time I made this post about how people see female singer-songwriters differently from male singer-songwriters, just to say there was a gendered aspect, and he ignored me for a whole afternoon and then proceeded to blow up at me on Messenger because he thought my post was 'in poor taste' or something. I don't know, it was bullshit. But that's the kind of thing he would do. He would put himself in charge of things and I would just be like, whatever."

When the girl finished talking, Jay's stunned silence was palpable.

"That feel good?"

She nodded and passed the baton.

Jay gestured toward the bottle of wine, which was on the ground next to my ankles. I took his cup from him and poured slowly, stopping just short of the rim. "That's enough, I hope?"

"Yes, ma'am." He swallowed, then sighed as if mulling something over. When he finished, he said, "You gotta get used to it—not that you should. But a lot of guys are angry."

"Yeah," I said. "I don't know about Cody though. I don't know that I would call him angry."

"Maybe not yelling-angry," said Jay. "Men have all of these things they feel like they're supposed to deal with by themselves, but the only thing they're taught how to do is get angry. So, they just get angry over shit, and then hopefully they eventually figure out some other way of coping. But until then, it's all anger. That's why you have guys starting fights for no reason, or punching walls or whatever."

"Or losing their mind over posts on Facebook."

"Yeah," he said.

"And you're speaking from experience?" I said. "I mean, you weren't angry."

Jay laughed darkly. "My dad died when I was eleven, and then my mom married a guy who treated both her and me like shit. Fuck yeah, I was angry. I was so angry for years."

"So then what happened?"

"I don't know." Jay was silent for a few seconds, thinking. "I don't know if anything happened. Maybe I'm still angry."

"You're like, the least angry," I replied, laughing. "You're not even aggressive."

"Wow, alright."

"What?"

"You don't think I can be aggressive!"

"I never said you *can't* be aggressive! Just that you haven't been aggressive toward me."

"Not yet, you mean," he joked.

I shrugged, laughing.

Jay's face was hard to make out in the dark, but I felt his foot slowly pass behind my left ankle, curling around my leg for a moment before a car rolled down the road and made us flinch. I took a fake drink from my near-empty cup, but I knew as the headlights passed over us that Jay could see the smile I'd tried to conceal inside it. He whistled quietly into the blackness ahead of us as the rumbling of the car grew more and more distant, and I thought, *There it is again that real-time nostalgia.*

Once the other car drove by, it wasn't long before Jay decided we should pack up for the night. We gathered up the cups and the remainder of the wine, and I handed them off to Jay, who loaded them back into the car.

There was a rush of heat as I got up from the bench, and I had to grab the back to get my bearings. I was drunker than I thought. I had no idea how long we'd been sitting there, not that it mattered. It was Friday. I had no reason to be up early the next morning. Sure, there was a hangover to be dealt with, there was Cody, the potential Exit Interview. But these things were all non-starters; they weren't real. I tried to imagine making it back to the apartment, stepping out of Jay's car, walking to the elevator, unlocking the door, but the idea seemed absurd. Not just the thought of doing them tonight, but that I had ever managed to do them, that anyone managed to do anything. It was all so much work.

I squinted at Jay's car. I hadn't paid much attention to our immediate surroundings, but now they were so loud, the lone streetlight that had hung over us all night suddenly offensive. Jay was already sitting in the driver's seat, scrolling on his phone, waiting. *Come on,* I thought to myself, *you just have to get in. Then you have a break. You don't have to make any other decisions.* It was like this thing I read once about how part of us craves being dead because we just get to rest, finally, after always having to decide things all the time. At the time I read it, it had seemed so morbid and dramatic. But now I finally understood what they'd been talking about. To just rest for five seconds—to close your eyes after a life of exhausting tasks and sink into the earth as the world melts off of you—it sounded so nice.

Then, somehow, I was in Jay's passenger seat, yanking the seatbelt over my lap as the Guard Dog glowered down from the dash.

"Hey, watch him," Jay said, gesturing at it as he turned the key in the ignition. "Items may shift during flight."

I nodded, snapping back into shape for a moment to smile at his joke. When I scooped up the dalmatian, it was cold. Soothing. I pressed it to my cheek.

"Am I taking you home?"

"Yeah," I said.

"Are you okay?"

"Yeah," I said again. It was a lie, but I was less concerned with the truth than the economy of words and energy. There was still the key, the elevator. I had to conserve.

Jay shot me a small, skeptical frown before returning his attention to the road. "You can open the window," he offered.

I said, "Okay," and then didn't open it.

ONE OF THE GREATS

The next morning, I didn't wake up so much as phase into consciousness. Like I'd been lying there half-dressed with my eyes open for hours, my body and brain fully alert short of their sensory functions, which had been unplugged. I wasn't particularly exhausted, somehow hardly hungover. I just wasn't convinced I'd slept at all. I got out of bed, stumbled to the bathroom to look in the mirror. To my surprise, I didn't look wiped out. My eyes weren't sunken, none of that up-too-late bloodshot vibe about them. Half-heartedly squeezing a small blob of toothpaste onto the brush, I couldn't help but feel like I'd gotten away with something. I'd certainly gone overboard at the park with Jay, and the hangover I deserved was nothing short of apocalyptic. And yet...

Brushed, rinsed, spat. I splashed water on my face, something I hardly did in the mornings. I even almost considered flossing. There was no denying my mind was stuck on the events of the night before, despite my attempts to nudge it back to friendlier terrain. But I didn't feel anxious, just distant. Like I had suddenly forgotten what it was like to wake up in my body, what sorts of things I usually did. My perspective had shifted such that I was a stranger to myself. When I finished the bathroom routine, I wandered into the kitchen, opening cupboards aimlessly like an actor uncommitted to the role. After some time, I managed to locate all of the materials required for a cup of coffee. As I sipped, the nature of my distraction began to reveal itself. I could suddenly recall all these old feelings.

It was always like this when I got close to new people. I could maintain a kind of detachment, a high, for days on end purely from getting to know someone new. Sometimes it happened the first time I spent time with someone and then never again: an isolated explosion. Sometimes it happened more like a slow burn. Sometimes I didn't feel it at all, and it could be assumed the person would never reach that golden tier of closeness. A friend, maybe, but never One of The Greats. I suppose the feeling was what normal people refer to as Chemistry. I couldn't make it happen for just anyone, but I could speed up the process if I wanted, create the ideal conditions. Certain situations brought out the right moods in people and led to the right kinds of conversations. Getting lost together in a strange place was one of them. Getting drunk and talking late into the night was another. To feel this way after meeting up with Jay for the Guard Dog only made sense.

Before that night, it had been such a long time since any of The Greats had revealed themselves to me, let alone done it so quickly. With Cody, I'd never even been able to make it happen, though I never stopped trying to force it. Most of my energy was spent placing the two of us in these different crucibles trying to set off a reaction. I'd never admitted this to anyone, but I even bought one of those cheesy books full of questions that are supposed to make people fall in love with each other. I would pick out ones I thought were especially interesting and float them at random, just one here and there during dinner or a long car trip. He was always a good sport. Sometimes, his answers were even interesting. But nothing he said ever moved the needle. I never felt anything new. We would spend long nights smoking and talking and drinking. I would pass out early in the morning, having learned everything there was to know about his inner world, and then wake up disappointingly lucid.

I took a deep breath and focused on finishing my coffee. This was no longer a safe train of thought. Cody was coming over later that night—the Exit Interview—and I would have to revisit those disappointments. Those disappointments were the real answer to the question of why I left, the closest thing to a concise explanation I would be capable of giving. I could say so, but it didn't seem right. To tell him these things would be to tell him, essentially, that I thought he had a boring personality. And to what end? It could very well have been me that was the broken one, the one who wasn't participating in our relationship correctly. Up until the day I broke things off, I'd carried a deep shame about being unhappy. Like this caricature of an idealistic, irrational woman, pining after this unidentifiable spark she claims to be missing. Four years of comfort and relative acceptance, and I was going to throw it away to chase a notion of compatibility I may as well have made up. I had no way of knowing that I would ever come to feel the things Cody had never been able to make me feel. Only that I was dissatisfied enough to fling the goalpost ahead of me and run.

I picked up my phone to make sure I hadn't missed an update from Cody. After the Chris Cornell phone call, I'd muted all of my notifications for his messages, so I had to check manually to see if he replied. It was weird, though. Despite the muting, I hadn't changed any of our other settings—not the custom chat colors, not the default emoji. His nickname in Messenger was still some inside joke whose origins I'd forgotten years ago. All of these relics of our closeness, and yet here I was, making plans to meet up for the last time. In a way, it was fitting. There was no resentment, no malice or grief, none of the obligatory negative feelings. I just didn't want to see him again.

But he hadn't replied. My only unread message was from Jay, who had asked how my morning had gone and what time Cody was showing up.

I replied, *Just got up, not really hungover but Something. and he hasn't said anything.*

Not four seconds after I sent my reply, Jay started typing. *Smart, he's got you on the hook all day,* he said. There was a pause and then he sent, *Sorry you're something*

I don't mind being something, I said.

Jay was taking a while to respond. I started to worry about my reference to feeling Something had made everything weird. He'd been minding his own business, grazing in a meadow, and I'd just come barreling towards him with my hand outstretched, chasing him back into the woods. He'd probably reached the highway by now, where he was about to pop out of the trees and be mowed down by a tractor-trailer. 'Hey, mom, what's that thing on the side of the road?' 'Oh, well that used to be One of The Greats.'

I couldn't look at my phone anymore. I threw it onto my bed and chugged the rest of my coffee before stepping into the shower. When I got out, Jay had said, *Fair enough. I'm out with Tom today but call if you need backup.*

Still wrapped in my towel, I waddled out to the kitchen and took a photo of the Guard Dog, which had been sitting on the counter since the night before. I sent the photo to Jay and added, *I already have a backup.*

Jay didn't open my message right away, a sign he was busy and would be for a while. I placed my phone face-down on the counter and wandered back into my room to get dressed. The shower had taken the edge off my buzz, and I was beginning to feel more like a person. This was a stroke of luck, considering the task I had ahead of me. I dug through my clothes, trying to find something to wear for the Exit Interview whenever it was, exactly, that Cody planned on showing up. Despite its relative importance, putting an outfit together for this occasion took a fraction of the time it'd taken to get ready for the cemetery the week before. Then again, I'd chosen essentially the same outfit — the exact midpoint of looking sloppy and trying too hard, though this time for different reasons. If Jay's insights about how these things usually went held any water, I didn't want Cody to think he had some chance of winning me over. I couldn't look too attractive *or* too sad.

I'd already gathered most of Cody's things in a big box. He hadn't left behind much, despite his frequent weekend stays at my apartment. His detritus mostly consisted of single socks and laptop peripherals — AUX and USB cables whose purposes were unknown to me. One of the only items of particular interest was a set of little bamboo sushi rolling mats. A year or so ago one of

Cody's friends' girlfriends threw him a birthday party at a fish-shop after hours. She had an in with one of the owners, and they held a sushi-making class for all of us. The roll I made had turned out terrible, but Cody had enjoyed himself so much that I'd ended up buying the mats for him as a gift. We'd kept them in a drawer in my kitchen, planning to eventually bust them out and try making sushi again. I'd figured it could be another one of those crucibles, perhaps the fun adventure that would distinguish him as One of The Greats. We'd never gotten around to doing it, though, and, for all our good intentions, the set of mats was still in its packaging when I fished it out of the box to read the label. I spun it around in my hand, letting a sigh escape. One of the many aspects of our relationship that had never quite panned out. At least this one had only cost me $12.

When I checked my phone again, Cody still hadn't messaged me. I decided I would go for a walk. There were still dishes in the sink that needed washing, but I didn't care. Even after the shower, I was too uncomfortable to loiter around my apartment. Besides, I couldn't waste my most neutral outfit. I stepped out of my building and turned left. I didn't do much exploring in my neighborhood on my own, but I knew in that direction there were some restaurants and maybe a coffee shop. Maybe I could sit there for a few hours and dick around on my phone, fraying my nerves with espresso.

It didn't take me long to regret leaving home without my headphones. Walking by myself with no actual destination felt like some kind of obscure exception for which I had to answer, and I couldn't remember the last time I'd left the apartment by myself for a reason other than work. That was one of the advantages of being with Cody; I rarely had to do things alone. If there was something I wanted to do or see, I could just wait until the weekend when he and I were together. I never had to be that girl sitting alone in the window of a Starbucks pretending to read a book. Up until this weekend, I'd managed to insulate myself from this drastic change in circumstances, but with Jay tied up with Tom, and Sidney off doing who-knows-what, I was now doomed to spend time alone with my thoughts.

I turned a corner and made my way toward a row of restaurants. Not exactly unique city-living fare—there was a Five Guys, a Chipotle, some generic sports bar. These were the kind of places college kids went with their friends for a late hungover lunch after staying out until the morning, and sure enough, they were out there in droves. Though the cold weather had begun to roll in, more than a few groups were filling out the various sections of outdoor seating. I stared at them as I passed, trying not to make eye contact. I was thinking pathetic thoughts, possessed by this weird longing to be One of Them: to be happy in whatever relative way that they were. I could still remember a time when I was one of those people laughing with my friends outside a Five Guys, feeling not at all fortunate and probably thinking about how much everything sucked and how much work I had to get finished before the weekend was over. But as I walked past all of those tables packed tightly with reboots of my former friends, the gulf between those days and my current circumstances felt impossible. Only 22 and I had already become that annoying person languishing about how they wish they'd Enjoyed Their Youth.

I kept walking until I found a Starbucks. If I couldn't avoid this feeling no matter where I went. I preferred to experience it somewhere quieter than a Five Guys at peak hours. The place was nearly empty, most likely because their core demographic had decided to spend their afternoon at any and every other establishment in a three-block radius. The barista greeted me as soon as I entered, and I flinched, feeling caught off-guard by the acknowledgment that I was a real person and not some flimsy outline doomed only to observe.

"Hey," I nearly shouted back. I made my way up to the counter and ordered a caramel macchiato, my heart thumping at a rate that alarmed me.

The barista smiled, pushed a chunk of floppy, overgrown fringe out of his eyes. He looked slightly younger than me, like early-college age. My mind immediately began plotting out the backstory. He was a student at the same college as the hungover Five Guys kids. His major was probably English or something humanities-related—not because of the barista cliché but because of the way he was carrying himself. But while the hungover Five Guys kids had gotten to stay up until two or three in the morning getting drunk in some random guy's apartment, this barista had to be asleep early for work the next morning. And now, while all of his peers were a few blocks away, huddled over a too-small mesh table and throwing french fries at pigeons, he was stuck serving a caramel macchiato to this weird, washed-up chick who looked like she was about to have a panic attack. In that way, he related to my loneliness. "Good choice," he said. Maybe I was fishing, but he seemed to be speaking with sincerity, something a cut above the usual food-service politeness. He believed I had made a good choice of beverage.

"Thanks," I said.

After he punched my order into the computer he asked for my name. When I told him what it was, he grinned again and nodded.

"Is that with an *i* or a *y*?" he asked.

"It's an *i*," I said. "Nobody ever asks that."

"It's an important question!"

I thought and almost said the words 'A man after my own heart!' but decided to move off to the side instead and wait for my drink at an acceptable distance. I didn't want to overstay my welcome and become that weird customer who mistakes basic politeness for genuine interest in talking to me. I was surprised when, even at this distance, he looked up from making my coffee to continue the conversation.

"Midterms next week. You ready?"

"Oh," I said, "I'm not in school."

"No? What do you do?"

His eyes were bright and expectant, betraying a level of interest that nobody had shown towards something as mundane as my day job in a long time. I remembered being a student and the curiosity I once felt toward people like me, who were older and had graduated or otherwise gotten out. Always wanting to know what they were doing with their lives now, desperate for some prognostic insight about the person I would become in a few years, what it would be like to be someone with prospects, someone making money and living a more Adult and varied life.

I laughed. "Just, like, data entry. Nothing that exciting."

"Aw," he said. He looked up at me with concern as I stepped forward, making my way back toward the counter. "Don't say that. I don't even know what that is. It's exciting for me." A grin began to melt across his face when our eyes met, and I felt my face match it. It was this weirdly genuine moment. There was nothing flirty or meet-cute about it. I'd walked in eager to have my existence acknowledged, and he'd acknowledged it. I would never know for sure if he'd been sincere or just skilled at sincerity, but his words and gestures were hitting all of the right spots.

"I'm not being modest," I said. "It's literally, just..." I was watching my tone here, careful not to soil this interaction with sarcasm. "...inputting data into a spreadsheet. It's fine."

"Ah." The barista pouted, and I could tell he was a bit disappointed, if not with my attitude than with the fact that his probing had failed to yield any profound insights. He picked my cup up off of the counter and handed it to me, perking up a bit as my drink changed hands. "At least you don't have homework, though, right?"

"Yeah," I said. I smiled at him, a kind of recovery move. Don't worry, this all still kind of worth it. Life will get better for you after this. Or if not, at least you won't have to do homework.

"Have a good one."

"You too," I nodded up at him and pivoted to walk out. After a few steps, I called behind me, "Good luck!"

"What?"

"You said something about midterms?"

The barista laughed. "Oh, yeah," he said, "I'm not in school either. I just thought you were."

"Oh, okay. Thanks anyway."

Standing outside of the Starbucks in the sun, the weight of that weird interaction melting off me, I decided to check my phone. It had to have been almost an hour by now, right? Or half an hour? Or some reasonable length of time? There was a chance Cody had gotten back to me by now. But I had no new messages — no update from Cody and, somehow just as disappointing, no response from Jay, either. I thought for a second about calling him, taking him up on his offer. He'd said he was available in an emergency, and this felt close enough. I had no idea when Cody was coming, and my discomfort was at emergency levels. But the idea of him standing with a friend on a street across town somewhere and picking up the phone to hear me whining that I couldn't stand to be alone for a single afternoon was embarrassing. Besides, what he'd said was to call if I needed backup, the implication being that I would only need it when Cody was there.

I considered maybe just sending him another message. Or checking our conversation, at least, to see if he'd opened my last one. Something. I needed confirmation from some familiar person that I existed. But I was wary of tipping the balance. The thing with the barista had made me feel obscure and tired, like something to be pitied or appeased. I wanted to talk to Jay, but if I needed him now it would become a thing where I always needed him. And I was just beginning to get over always needing Cody. Are you so afraid, I thought, of blank space, your own company?

I'd never had a gap before, a significant period of just Not Needing. It simply wasn't done. But even as I reached this conclusion, deciding to stuff my phone away for at least another hour before inflicting myself on another person, the thought was still there. Just say hi or check-in, say something funny, say something else about the Guard Dog, the barista—it was less curiosity and more compulsion, a burning need.

Unable to bear the thought of my apartment, I continued walking the streets. I'd never felt the weight of my phone so distinctly: a useless brick against my thigh, not capable of giving me any of the things I needed. Maybe after finishing the macchiato, I could hole up in some restaurant. Someplace with a bar, maybe. I could be that woman at the end of the bar, not needing or wanting anyone, taking tiny sips of merlot from a glass that somehow never dips below half full. But that was the problem, I could never just do something. I could never shake the metacognition. If I was standing in line to order a sandwich, there was a sepia-toned cinematic playing in my head of a woman standing in line to order a sandwich, overdubbed with the thoughts of her onlookers commenting on her clothes or waxing poetic about some backstory they imagined. No action was too mundane; there was no escaping the movie. I could be sitting on the toilet and still gazing at the stills in a locket photo, imagining the other people discussing the woman who excused herself from the table. 'What a cool person, how did you meet her again?' I imagined that other people could just walk somewhere, grab a seat in a restaurant, and not be thinking, *I am a woman walking on the street. Now I'm sitting in a restaurant.* That's probably why they managed to do these things so easily—they weren't concerned about the blocking.

While I was walking, I didn't know where to look. Looking at the ground was a hazard, but I felt too volatile for eye contact. Every time I passed someone, I made a deliberate effort to avoid their eyes. At one point, I slipped up, and some woman stopped me to ask for directions to a bus terminal I'd never heard of. My sense of direction was nonexistent even for places I had heard of, so I lied and told her I was just a tourist. "Really just seeing the sights myself." Somehow not a total lie. She continued on her way with this vague look of disappointment, like she didn't believe me. Maybe because this wasn't a particularly touristy area, or because I looked too frazzled to be on vacation.

I felt the woman's eyes on me as I waited for the light to change and crossed the street, playing the movie in my head the whole time. The woman was continuing on her way without my directions, desperate not to miss her bus. But even as she hurried down the street, her eyes peeled for some other stranger who might be able to help her, she was stuck on the weird girl on Cherry St. who'd claimed to be a tourist. What kind of vacation could she be on? Where was she going? What kind of coffee was that? Why did she look like, if someone made direct eye contact for more than five seconds, she'd die where she was standing?

Another sign I'd met One of The Greats was that my mind would begin to change its approach to these movies. They'd start to have an audience of one person in particular. I walked a few more blocks and ducked into a random Mexican restaurant, rushing to the far end of the bar while I still had the guts. The place was nearly empty—a couple sharing a late lunch of nachos at a table near the front window; the waitstaff enjoying their downtime in a small huddle toward the back.

The bartender made his way over to me and asked me what I wanted. I'd never ordered wine from a bar before, but I was dead set on my ideal of the Woman Alone, who was always holding a glass. After some confusing back-and-forth in which the bartender informed me I had to choose which specific brand of merlot I wanted, he disappeared and returned with the cheapest one they had. The headache began to set in at the first swallow. I'd had my fair share of cheap wine, but this was overtly poison. Still, I couldn't deny that I'd created a mood. This much was clear to me as I sat back in my chair and pivoted to look at my surroundings. A woman sitting alone at a bar in a Mexican restaurant choking down the world's most transcendently shitty wine, soon to be paired with an order of guacamole, on this, the eve of her ex-boyfriend's Exit Interview. She was waiting for a different man—one who was twice her age—to text her back. I couldn't see them, but the two people on a date across the room were looking at me, turning their heads in shifts to not make it obvious. 'What a weird person. How long has she been nursing that same glass of wine?' Then, in the back row, if you squinted hard enough, Jay was laughing open-mouthed at me, toasting a Solo cup of wine, just kind of holding it up.

I didn't check my phone the entire time I was eating the chips. It had become this little betting game I was playing with myself: an endurance test. I was seeing how long I could go before trying to re-up on personal attention. And besides, being too attached to my phone would have ruined the scene. The people-watching at home don't want to see you obsessing over your Facebook Messenger inbox; they want you to sit there in your air of mystery, looking completely self-possessed. By the time I finished eating, I'd had enough of the role play and was looking forward to returning to my life, hopefully with a clearer idea of when Cody would be showing up.

But, as you might expect, there was nothing from either Jay or Cody, and when I got back onto the sidewalk I made it a few blocks before realizing I was being slowly pulled back in the direction of my apartment. I couldn't occupy myself for much longer unless I felt like spending even more money I didn't have on treats I didn't need or want. What was there to do walking around the city like this besides eat? There was sitting in a park and reading. That was always an option, though I couldn't recall ever seeing anyone outside of a romantic comedy do it.

As if in direct response to all of my existential languishing about what to do with the rest of my afternoon, some kind of art festival thing had popped up in a plaza near my building. It was the sort of thing that probably happened all the time. I was just never out to notice them. I only ever crossed through this plaza on workdays, when it was occupied by people on their lunch breaks horking down Au Bon Pain and swatting away pigeons. Today, though, all of the wire tables and chairs had been moved and replaced with a series of pop-up booths selling necklaces, scarves, blown glass, all of this art. It looked vaguely interesting, and as I passed through, I found myself strangely compelled to participate.

I stopped at one of the less-crowded booths where an older woman was selling jewelry. Within a minute, I was drawn to these distressed-looking metal rings with animal heads on them. A deer, a wolf, an elephant. Potential friends for the Guard Dog. I lifted one from the display to look at it closer. It was a tiger in mid-roar, striped with dark engravings. As I turned it around in my hand, I could feel the older woman looking at me, calculating in her head the likelihood of purchase. It didn't bother me, though, only made my presence feel less intrusive.

"Do you make these?" I asked eventually, gesturing down at the set of rings.

She laughed softly. "No, I'm not that talented. We source everything from different local artists. All of the blown glass on the other side is by this man who has his own studio in the South Side. Featuring them helps give them exposure, so we try to have a rotation of different artists in the area." Her speech was slow and full of gesticulation, as if she was being deliberately patient with me, sensed my lack of experience with Art like this. If so, she was right. "I do make wire sculptures from time to time."

"Oh, cool," I said, not knowing what else to say.

She nodded. "So, these you're looking at are $14. There are also pendants over there for $20." The woman pointed toward a similar display a few feet to my right, her long, kitschy earrings clacking and swinging as she moved.

"Oh, okay." I looked back down at the ring, pretending to be considering my options. I hadn't come here pretending to buy something, and I wasn't flush with cash. I had planned to make some small talk and then disappear back into the crowd. I was just passing through. But when I tuned back into my surroundings, I realized I was one of the only truly engaged patrons left browsing at her booth and that her blue-lidded eyes were pointed at me in a forceful, but not at all malicious, sort of way. I knew if I left without buying something, I'd feel guilty all day. "I think I'll take this," I said. The Guard Dog was getting a friend after all.

"Good!" The woman retrieved the ring from my hand and wandered over to another area on the inner side of the booth to wrap it up. As I dug around in my wallet, I watched her plump hands fold and pinch and fold until the ring was secured in a neat bundle of thin white tissue. This woman wrapped up animal rings the way Sidney rolled joints.

We made the exchange—fourteen bucks for the little white pouch and a small card detailing the name of the seller and the artist. "Thank you," I said.

"You too, honey."

On my way through the plaza, I didn't stop at any of the other booths. I was officially too broke to afford anything else that might catch my eye. I held the ring and card gently in my hand as I walked, thumbing the details of the tiger's mouth. I hadn't been in love with the ring, but I was coming around. It had a nice weight. I imagined that having it on my finger would be satisfying, give me some kind of weird power. Maybe that was uncool in some way: an ignorant assumption about something exotic. Maybe it was because a punch with this thing could tear a person up.

When I left the plaza, I slowed down and pulled over against a building to read the card I'd been given. On one side was a description of the vendor, Red Lotus Designs, which was run by Cheryl—presumably the woman I'd just spoken to—and someone who looked like her daughter. On the flip side was a short bio of the artist, Lee Torres, who lived a few miles out of the city. The bio referred to her as an Artisan who had been an apprentice under some of the most respected living metallurgical artists in the country, including Amos Ong. Within a few sentences, I'd been tangled in this web of prestige I'd never realized existed. Established artists who made intricate sculptures out of metal mentoring slightly younger artists, ones who'd probably vied for the privilege to name-drop such notorious metallurgical rockstars as Amos Ong on their websites. As I unwrapped the ring from the paper, I could feel the decades of metal art dynasties unfolding behind me. I couldn't help but wonder if the same had been true for the Guard Dog. Someone, somewhere, had broken their back training under one famous ceramics artist, and so on, and so on. Then the Guard Dog was born—his sad, mottled face the culmination of a long and cut-throat ceramic art food chain. It was a trip to think about and inspired more passion than my prior image of a clearance shelf at Home Goods.

Things were good when I arrived at my apartment—card in my pocket, ring on my finger. I felt like I'd accomplished something if only the feat of spending a chunk of a single afternoon alone. On the way up to my floor, I felt the anxiety mounting, but I could manage. It wasn't crisis-level. Cody would text me soon. He would knock on the door, and when I let him in things would be weird, but they would end, and I would manage. And I could call Jay after. It was a comforting thought—his potential wisdom like a carrot dangling before me. Just do the Exit Interview and all will be well. Make it through.

Once I'd steadied myself as much as possible, I pulled out my phone to check for a message from Cody. It was a habit I'd repeated so many times by this point that I was no longer considering the possibility of him messaging me and letting me know he was on his way. But this time, the sole notification on my screen was not some pointless email or calendar update, but a single message from Cody himself that read: *be there in like an hour. is that good?*

yeah.

The outgoing message had barely completed its *wooshing* sound when I opened up my phone app and tapped Jay's name. He said I could call him for backup, and it was backup I needed. It rang four times, then patched me through to the generic female voiceover stating that the person I dialed had a voicemail box that had not been set up yet. I called a second time—the same result. Shrugging off my bag onto one of the kitchen chairs, I felt the soup of complimentary salsa, bile, and terror rising in my throat. An hour had never felt so long.

THE EXIT INTERVIEW

There were no buzzers in my building, so when Cody showed up, I had to go down and let him in myself. I got the all-important text—*here*—and then was transported inside the elevator, clenching my thumbs in my fists as it raced my stomach to the ground floor.

The only saving grace was having Jay inside my head, making it all pedestrian, a rite of passage. The Exit Interview—it's just something that happens, some indiscriminate phenomenon that can't help but play out. God knows how many Jay himself had participated in. What about the girls Jay dated in his 20's? Were they supposed to walk around for the rest of their lives feeling like monsters? To survive this, I would have to become a kind of anthropologist, a passive observer, my investments intellectual in nature and shallow in scope. I would have to change my entire personality, and I had the tail end of the world's shortest elevator ride to do it.

As soon as the elevator doors slid open, I could see him outside crying. It was like one of those movies where the guy shows up to the girl's door late at night in the pouring rain, ready to atone for whatever stupid thing he did, scoop her up in his arms, have a dimly-lit and chaste-looking sex montage. This was, in essence, my reality: a man outside my door in the dark willing to throw it all away for me and confess to any number of nonexistent crimes. Except I had no interest in progressing to the R&B bed montage. I wanted this to be over and for Cody to leave. I wanted to lay in my bedroom in peace and wait for Jay to text back.

I leaned my weight into the door, forcing it open enough for Cody to hold it and step forward into the light of the lobby.

I swallowed. "Hey."

"Hey," he breathed.

My impression had been correct. He was sniffling, flushed, and messy. I couldn't recall ever seeing him like this. I thought of the last time we spoke on the phone, right before Taco House. He was so curt then, still unwilling to peel back the veneer of the Guy in Charge. But the past few weeks had changed something. He'd molted and was laid bare, a hunk of wet guts heaving in a ring of torn plastic.

I didn't say anything as I walked over to the elevator and pressed the button on the wall, beginning our journey to my floor together for what I hoped would be the last time. I was avoiding Cody's eyes but could still hear his breaths catch in his throat on the way out.

"Can I just get a hug or something?" he said. "Please."

"I don't know," I said. I was being as flat as possible to spurn any attempt of his to make this exchange take any longer than it had to. I was invoking white bread, an unmarked box. "I don't think that's a good idea."

"Fine." He sniffled.

I stared at the wall, at nothing. The elevator filled the gaps with its unnerving clangs. When we reached the seventh floor, he exited before me, forcing me to brush past him to unlock the door and let us both in.

"You never have the AC on," he said.

"I'm always cold."

I was standing at the table with my back to him, my keys dangling from my index finger.

"Just do it already." Cody had managed to calm himself on the ride up to my floor but was once again falling apart. I didn't want to look at his face.

"Do what?" I said. "I don't know what you want me to say really. I'm sorry." I looped my finger through my keyring and dragged my keys in an infinity shape across the table, scraping the particleboard.

"Just tell me the actual reason."

"I don't know. I just think it's time."

"Wow," he said. I turned around just in time to see something change in his face, the wheel catching halfway between self-pity and righteous anger. "Five years –"

"Four."

"Whatever," he breathed. "Four years and all of a sudden it's just time? Okay."

I walked over to the other side of the room, sliding the tiger ring on and off my finger for something to do. I didn't reply to him. Jay's quick n' dirty pre-interview counseling hadn't prepared me for this much silence, the burden of having to provide empirical data for weeks' or even months' worth of baked-in feelings. I'd imagined this conversation as a kind of scene, separate from both of us. This notion that it would not proceed without intervention had been entirely lost on me. I felt tricked.

"I just don't really feel it."

"Feel what?"

I resisted the urge to throw up my hands. I could see through to the masochism at the heart of his question, the sleeping rage at its core waiting to be activated. But I wasn't going to provide that satisfaction.

"I don't know. I just don't think this is working anymore."

"And you didn't think to talk about it first?"

"Well, I guess this is us talking about it."

"But you don't even want to hear what I think," he exclaimed. Each of his sentences was a self-contained emotional arc spanning grief, resignation, anger. He wandered off through the door to my bedroom, his voice trailing off as he disappeared.

I followed behind, raising my voice. "I do care," I lied. "But there's nothing you can change to fix it."

When I caught up to Cody, he was on the bed, looking strangely small. I was reminded of how people in horror movies tend to make the mistake of running further into the house while being pursued, down into the basement, or toward a back room with no exit. There he was, folded over himself on what used to be his side of the bed, this simpering victim. I hated that.

I had the fantasy of myself as a benevolent dumper, facing Cody in my doorway with my eyes betraying just enough compassion, gentle, but firm—the boss that lets you go but won't make security drag you out. You get to take all the time you need to pack your things, mull the bittersweet memories as you place each trinket into the box, and think about what's next. And that sweet, sweet severance pay.

None of this happened. It was just these half-sentences, these long, weepy sighs. He looked up at me. We both began to speak at once, the sound of metal scraping metal.

"Do you even still love me?"

I looked past him. "I don't know."

"How do you not know?"

"I *have* a love for you. I just don't know if it's like that or—"

Cody's eyes had drifted somewhere behind me, causing his face to warp into one of horror and utter betrayal. Out of concern, I'd let myself trail off, turning around to see whatever had caught his attention. Upon the armoire, looking clean over the crown of my head, stood the dalmatian.

"What is that?" Cody stammered.

"What do you mean?" I said. "It's a dalmatian."

"Where did you get that from?" We made eye contact, and I suddenly understood the source of his rapidly increasing distress.

"I don't know," I said.

"Did someone get it for you? Who got it for you?"

"Nobody," I lied. "I found it."

"Where did you find it?"

"Outside."

"Where outside?"

"Don't worry about that," I said. "Do you still want to talk?"

"I just don't remember you ever having that."

I sat down next to him on the bed, something I'd been reluctant to do. But now, in the wake of his hyper-focus and weird panic, it felt necessary. Being next to me seemed to calm him a bit, to take the edge off of his breakdown. Still, I wondered how good this was for either of us. There was too much opportunity here to get too casual, to give him the wrong idea. But was there any place in this apartment that wasn't rife with this sort of emotional pitfall?

"Can you just give me one hug?" he asked between still-frantic breaths.

"I don't know if that's a good idea."

"You still care about me, though. Right?"

"Right. But this is just making it harder than it has to be."

Cody let out a mix between a sob and an exasperated sigh. "But it doesn't even have to be. You're just doing this for no reason. You're just depressed or something."

I inched away from him on the bed, somehow colder now than I'd already been. "No," I said. "I'm not."

"Then why are you just giving up on me for no reason?" His voice cracked again, and he hunched back over, pulling his sleeve over his hand to wipe his face amid full-body shudders.

I was unable to tell at this point if I hated seeing him like this, or just hated him, or hated the fact that my years of trying in vain to reach him had somehow culminated in him weeping over my lack of tact and me sitting here watching it like a robot. It was a cruel reversal of the hard work I'd once been so happy to put in for us, bending myself into whatever form would evoke some kind of compassion from him, digging every single day, thanklessly, through a new stratum of rock, all to reach some kind of core—one that wouldn't appear until I'd already given up on the prospect entirely, admitted to us both how futile the whole exercise was. Reluctantly, I leaned in, hugged him while thinking to myself that it was the last he was getting from me. It was unwieldy, the physics of each other's bodies suddenly and inexplicably alien to us. Even the way he smelled was unfamiliar: musty and old-man-like like he had expired. He let out what seemed to be a cleansing breath, and then let go, looking more stable but drained of energy. He'd gone white.

"You good?" I asked.

"Yeah," he said. "I just feel, like, not right. Dizzy."

"Did you eat today?" Here it was, I was being pulled right back in again—the universal solver of problems.

"No."

"Do you want anything?"

"I guess."

"Cheerios?"

I was washing Cody's bowl in the sink when Jay called. He'd just left, and the apartment felt especially empty, like the prom room in a hotel after the lights go back on. I had no idea how I was supposed to sleep that night and, later, return things to their former state. When my phone went off, I wished that Jay would invite himself over, or better yet, pick me up and take me somewhere else.

"Hey," I said.

"Are you okay?"

"Oh." I let out this weird, tired laugh, recalling that I'd been pestering him all day to come to provide backup. He probably thought I was dead. "Yeah, I'm fine."

"What happened?"

"I made him Cheerios."

"So, what? You made up?" There was a hint of disappointment in his voice.

"No, he just needed something. I don't know. I thought he was going to go into a diabetic coma if he didn't eat something."

"He's diabetic?"

"No."

There was a pause.

"How long was he there?"

"Like an hour." As I spoke, I paced around the apartment, looking for things I could clean up or fix. On the bedside table, a near-empty water glass that Cody had used while eating next to me in silence. "It was weird."

"Always is."

"No, like," I dumped the backwash from the glass. "He was upset."

"You didn't expect that?"

"No!"

Jay didn't say anything.

"I swear to god that was the most emotion he showed in our entire relationship. He kept bursting into tears and asking me to give him a hug and shit. It was so weird."

"Did you give him a hug?"

"No," I lied.

"Good. That's always a move, in my experience."

"A move?"

"Yeah," Jay said. "Like, you give them a hug, and then before you know it, you're comforting them and taking back everything you said, taking back the whole breakup, and then you end up sleeping together or something."

"Oh," I said. "God. No. No moves."

"Good."

"He saw the Guard Dog."

"Oh?"

"Yeah. It freaked him out for some reason. He kept asking me where I got it from."

"And did you tell him?"

"No," I said. "Why, is that also a move?"

"No, he probably thinks the dog was a move."

"By you?"

"Yeah, by me."

THE FOUNTAIN

Jay insisted we get dinner the following evening. This was fine with me. Even after a passable night's sleep, I felt uncomfortable being in the apartment. On the phone, Jay had told me about his friend who had a rule about always burning sage after breakups. As knocked-loose as I felt after escorting Cody out of my building, I'd thought this was a little bit over-the-top. And then the morning rolled around, and I saw the cartoon green lines oozing out of the mattress where his slumped-over, expired sweat had been fermenting.

"I don't have sage, but I have the address of some really good Italian food," said Jay, laughing a little as I adjusted my seatbelt in the passenger seat.

"I like Italian food."

"I had my suspicions."

He had the radio turned to some nothing static station, so we sat in relative silence as the car stop-started with violent jerks. This part of the city was busy for a Sunday night. Whatever art showcase I'd passed through the day before appeared to be part of some bigger event that had closed off every intersection in the city, aside from the one that we were attempting to clear. The last car still ahead of us swerved around the corner just as the light changed to red, and Jay hurried for the brake, causing us both to lurch forward then slam against the headrests. At the next green light, he planned on making a break for it, only to be hindered by a group of tourist-looking women half-sprinting down the crosswalk.

"Fuck," Jay said.

"I love the weekends."

"Remind me again why I'm always the one driving."

"I don't have a driver's license."

"Ha."

"No," I said. "I'm serious."

"Wait, you actually can't drive?"

"I can." I grinned, feeling his smirk on me. "I just shouldn't. Seeing as I'm not licensed."

He turned to me with this perplexing little grin. "How did I not know this about you?"

"You didn't ask."

In a way, I was as confused as he was. It hadn't been that long, but even so, there was so little Jay had learned about me.

"Well," he turned his focus back to the road, taking us, finally, across the intersection. "We'll have to fix that. I can't do this every weekend."

"Who says I want to see you every weekend?"

"You," Jay said, "so far. This weekend, last weekend, the weekend before that—"

"That one doesn't count."

"And why is that?"

"I didn't even know you. You were just there."

"Ah." For the last few beats, he'd been speaking with a lilt, a kind of uptalk that bordered on sultry. And now, turning to me in a dull moment on the road sent all the built-up tension out in my direction, a pulse of deep pink light so brief I could have missed it. "Well, we were together."

"Yes."

"And it was a weekend."

"Yes."

"And you enjoyed yourself."

Another pulse, a flash. Between glances through the windshield, he was looking down his nose at me, the corner of his mouth slightly raised in the way I'd come to recognize as familiar—the way he'd done it in the car and at the cemetery; standing in the kitchen at Sidney's, the light above as harsh as a supermarket; and the next day through the crack in the door. Picturing this, I didn't know what I wanted. There was a mood I couldn't access, but it was so warm. I grinned, trying to push down this nameless heat. I wondered if my face betrayed any of these feelings. "Yes," I said.

"Well, then I think it counts."

"Maybe it does."

We were free now, a solid few blocks away from whatever event had slowed us down, and the radio was still pumping out static. This, coupled with the fact that Jay was now driving a bit faster, created a feeling of oddly pleasant unease, of being just slightly out of control. The lack of a melody to anchor to made me realize I'd barely listened to music at all, lately, unless I was with Jay.

"I hope you like this place," Jay said, coaxing me back into my body. "Comfort food."

"I could use that."

"I figured as much."

We had already reached the inevitable part of the journey where it felt as if we'd phased out of the tri-state area. We were always in the city and yet an impossible distance from it, in another time or hooked into the wrong set of ports, receiving the wrong information, a temporary break from the timeline. Maybe if I went by myself to that restaurant where I'd bought us both margaritas, it wouldn't even be there—a 7-11 and a Verizon store and an under-construction Wendy's filling its place. There were stars out—not many, but more than seemed possible, more than I'd normally see.

A few more minutes and we were there. Jay pulled into one of the five or so parking spaces set against the side of the building.

"This is us," he said.

We walked in, and I immediately felt comfortable. This was the sort of place I'd been before, where I knew how to behave. Italian food and loud people laughing. Dark paneling and vertical floral wallpaper yellowed either by design or by cigarette smoke over years, maybe decades. It looked like the kind of place a distant family member might have rented out for a birthday or christening, inexplicably inviting my father even though we hadn't spoken with them in years.

"This is the real deal," I said.

"You're damn right."

We stood at the podium. As we waited, I slid my foot back and forth on the musty pink mudroom carpet, watching it go light and then dark again. A few minutes later, we were led to our seats by a woman who looked like she could have been my cousin. She didn't look like me, but maybe like the image my parents had probably had in their heads shortly after my conception: olive skin and sleek raven hair that reached her mid-back.

"They have these giant meatballs," Jay said, taking the world's longest glance at the menu before closing it back up and holding it shut with crossed hands. "Highly recommend."

"Hm," I said. "Kind of want pasta though."

"Get both."

"No!"

"Why not?"

"Um, money?"

"I'm buying." His eyes glistened with self-satisfaction. Warm, pink light.

Not sure what to say, I exhaled and went back to looking at the menu.

"Don't pout," Jay said. "Just accept."

I looked back up at him and rolled my eyes, suppressing a grin. "I think I want the linguini."

"Linguini and a big meatball it is."

We were both quiet for a while. I continued perusing the menu despite already knowing what I wanted. It was there; it was something to look at. You could tell by the menu that this place was the authentic—the absolute real deal—of tacky Italian-American cuisine. None of the entrees were in Italian. There was no pretense; they weren't trying to pass themselves off as especially fancy or culturally aware. Just big-ass meatballs and squeaky plastic upholstery in the booths—a place owned by, or at least named after, someone's grandma.

"Sorry I'm not talking much," I said eventually.

Jay's expression quickly softened, betraying whatever bravado he'd been trying on in some not-entirely-unsuccessful effort to charm me. "No, that's okay. I figured you were kind of fried after..."

"Yeah," I said. "Thanks."

"You know I'm proud of you."

"Thanks."

"That's not an easy thing. I've been there. Especially when they keep asking questions."

"And insist that you hug them."

"Yeah," Jay said, brushing the palm of his hand backward across his head. "If I have one critique for next time, it'd be to keep it short. Don't let it even get to that point."

"Easier said than done when they're literally crying and shit on the edge of your bed."

"Wait—" Jay was laughing a little. "You let him in your bedroom?"

I pursed my lips. "What am I supposed to do? He's not a pet hamster. I'm pretty sure he can go where he wants."

"Okay, then. I take it back. I have two critiques. "

"Shut up." Now we were both laughing. "It's not like it would change anything. I wasn't going to take him back."

"It's for the best," he said as if to convince me.

"Yeah," I said. "I know."

There was a brief pause in our conversation as the waitress took our drink orders—two glasses of red, apparently on Jay. I considered telling him about the day I'd had leading up to Cody's arrival: the art booths, the long walk, the Merlot I'd been too disgusted to even finish. But I already knew his reaction would expose me, my stupidity, my frazzled enmeshment with him that was, at best, way too soon. He would say 'Why did you go to a Mexican restaurant and order Merlot? That's your first problem. Nobody does that.' And I would have to muster some response other than 'Because I wanted to hang out with you and you weren't around and seeing you the other night had made me forget everything I swear I knew before about being a person, and I don't know why.' There was no way I would be able to get around saying those things. It simply couldn't be done. So instead, I kept talking about Cody and the Exit Interview, though I didn't want to do that, either.

"He kept insinuating that there was still time to fix everything. Like there was still time to discuss. And I was like, this relationship isn't a democracy."

"Damn."

"No, like, I didn't say that, but I was thinking it."

"Yeah, I know."

"Like, he kept acting as he could just change somehow, and I would suddenly be happy again. I felt like we weren't even talking about the same thing. He was talking about our relationship like there was a protocol that I wasn't following like somehow, I wasn't even breaking up with him correctly. And I was like, 'Have you ever heard of feelings?' I don't know."

Jay snorted, repeating me under his breath. "Have you ever heard of feelings?"

"I finally was like, 'There's nothing you can change.' It sounds like a Disney Channel movie but he was, like, acting like he still wanted to be with me, and I was like, 'How? I'm not even me.'"

The waitress set our glasses down in front of us and we paused our conversation once again for the obligatory round of thank-yous. We ordered: linguini for me, a big meatball for Jay, and, at his insistence, a second one to share.

I took my first sip and said, "It just always felt like a performance around him. Even last night."

"You're not at the fountain," Jay said. He took a sip and, sensing my confusion, held up a hand to signal he'd continue. "You have to go to the fountain."

I narrowed my eyes.

"I have this friend, Anna," he continued. "She reads tarot cards and has a little side business where she makes self-help videos and puts them on YouTube."

"So, she's a life guru."

"I know, but listen. She has this thing she talks about called the fountain." He took another quick sip while I waited, perplexed. "Have you ever been to a zoo or an amusement park?"

"Yes?" I looked around the room, suddenly self-conscious that people walking by or sitting in our vicinity were hearing this.

"Right, so you're at a zoo, you're with a big group of people, and you all split up, but you have to pick a spot to meet in case one of you gets lost. So, you say, 'Okay, let's all meet at the fountain.'"

"Okay."

"And now if you get lost, you don't want to just wander around looking for the rest of the group. Because where are they all going to be? Where do they know you're supposed to meet? At the fountain. Are you with me?"

"Sure," I said. "But what does this have to do with me. Who am I supposedly meeting?"

"It doesn't matter. The point is that you're never going to find your people if you don't stick by the fountain. Whoever, or whatever, is coming for you, they are going to one place, and you need to be there in that place. That's the idea"

"And you're saying Cody isn't at the fountain."

"I'm saying maybe he was at the fountain, and maybe now he's walking away from it. Maybe he'll come back to the fountain eventually, and then both of you will be like, 'Oh shit, okay.' But for right now, he's where he is and you feel drawn somewhere else. And you need to stay in that place."

"So, basically what I said."

"What you said, yeah. You said he wants to be with you."

"But I'm not even me."

"Right. But it keeps going. Let's say we walk out of here, and I take you home, and you meet this other guy. He understands what you're trying to say. He just gets everything. And he doesn't judge you. He has good taste in music, he buys you dinner, he holds open doors for you. He drives..."

"A beat-up '02 Honda Accord?" I interjected, referencing the car parked outside the restaurant.

Jay was frazzled for a second, embarrassed by the insinuation that he'd referenced himself. "No," he said, "no. He drives, like, a non-shitty car. And he looks like Tom."

"Like Tom?"

"Tom is hot."

"Are you sure about that?"

Jay shook his head, laughing at me. "No taste."

"Uh-huh."

"So, you meet this guy, and he's perfect, or whatever. He's your dream man."

I pretended to retch silently, lifting my fingers to my mouth to hold back the imaginary bile.

"And you love him so much, and he's great, and you're having a really great time at the fountain together, and you're thinking, 'Okay, this must be it. Everything is perfect. We'll be happy forever.' And then one day he wants to go somewhere else, move on, change all of a sudden. And even though the things he wants are not you, and you know that you feel compelled to follow him. So, do you do it?"

"No? Yes?"

"No," Jay said with sudden seriousness. "Because you're already at the fountain, and he's trying to take you away from it. It doesn't matter how much you think you love him or whatever, or how many awesome restaurants he takes you to, or whatever. You have to stay at the fountain."

"Why?"

"Because that's where you need to be when they find you."

I laughed with a kind of exasperation that I'd been trying to hide but had made known. "But, like, why? Who?"

Jay smirked and finished the last of his wine, smacking his lips after it went down. "I don't know," he said. "I didn't make it up. That's just what she said."

"Do you believe in it, though?"

"As much as I believe in anything, I guess." He shrugged.

"So, you think you're there now?"

"At the fountain, you mean?"

"I don't know." He chuckled. "I've been here a hell of a long time, so I hope so. Then I'd at least be doing something right."

"Ah."

"What about you?"

Jay looked at me and I felt something, a weight.

"Maybe," I said.

PINK MEAT

When we got to Jay's place, I wasn't thinking about sex. I was thinking about dinner. I was thinking about whether the Styrofoam container of linguini I'd brought back from the restaurant would go bad if I could leave it sitting in the front seat all nigh—bullshit calculations in my head based on the temperature outside and some food safety course I'd taken for one of my jobs back in college. The cutoff temperature where food starts to become unsafe and grow microorganisms is roughly 34 degrees; it's supposed to hover a bit under that for the rest of the night, making the car almost like a refrigerator, right? So, whatever.

It wasn't that I was totally opposed to sleeping with him—I knew he wasn't. I just wasn't giving it weight. There were moments here and there where tension spilled, little doors that would creak open, but I would walk by them. The occasional banter boiling over. Something weird arcing between us as he drove, when we were both a little drunk. Our ankles brushing that one night we drank merlot out of Solo cups at the park. But they were flashes, just theoretical. They weren't places I wanted to go.

The only tell was his front door. Up to this point, every guy I'd fucked had some weird door thing. The front door of Cody's house would make a small beep when you opened it; there was some kind of security system, and I'd have to cough over the sound when I was sneaking in. Tall Joe's house was so cramped the couch was pushed up against the front door, so to get in you had to walk around the side of the house and enter through the kitchen. Short Joe, you jiggled the handle, and Drew was Short Joe's roommate, so same. I only blew Hot Joe from high school, and both times it was in his car, but he'd have to unlock the passenger side for me whenever he pulled around to pick me up and always forgot. Everyone I'd fucked, there was some extra step involved—a prolonged process of getting in or out. It was a well-established pattern by this point.

When we reached the door of Jay's apartment, he held it open for me, then told me to pull it towards me and push it back out to make sure it was "clicked-in" and would stay shut. I did what he asked, not noticing because I wasn't trying to notice. I was still thinking the thoughts of a friend, someone who dealt only in flashes and was mostly concerned with the Styrofoam container of leftover linguini waiting for me in his front seat. The front door of the apartment opened directly to a steep, narrow staircase leading up to his actual living space, where a chubby tortoiseshell cat glowered down at us. Jay reached the top and bent down, gave the cat a few scratches behind the ear, introduced it to me as Patti Smith. *Fine,* I thought.

He led me over to the couch and then disappeared down a narrow hallway. I pulled my keys and wallet from my coat pocket and placed them on the glass table in front of me. The whole apartment had this kind of just-been-cleaned, lemony smell to it which played interestingly off of the otherwise-very-dingy surroundings. The room was dull and constricting—knobby, forest green carpet, and dark wooden furniture. Shelving units stretched from floor to ceiling on either side of me, packed tightly with vinyl records. Every time I saw this much of anything in one place, a big collection of video games or music or movies, my first thought was that most of the things I was looking at were only really intended to be displayed, not used. I wondered how many of the records Jay had actually listened to and how many hadn't been so much as pulled off the shelf since he'd bought them. In front of me was a small TV sitting on a rickety-looking stand. The screen was covered in a thick layer of dust, likely having been neglected in favor of the laptop that sat on the glass coffee table directly in front of me, open but not on. It occurred to me that, despite having never been to his place before, I had imagined— on multiple occasions—what it would look like. And for the most part, I had been correct.

Jay reappeared in the doorway beside the couch, holding a bottle of Canadian Club and two Styrofoam cups.

"Pulling out the stops for me, I see," I joked.

"Are you not impressed?" Another flash, but only that.

I scooted over, and Jay sat down beside me. He filled up both of the Styrofoam cups—big pours—then set the bottle down beside his feet. I sipped and wanted to wince but tried not to. Jay was cool enough, but there was still always this thing with whiskey: this weird pressure to prove that you weren't too much of a lady or delicate flower to tolerate it. I didn't want to care about this thing; I was aware of how sexist it was, but it was still there, demanding some kind of response or lack-there-of. My face scrunched involuntarily, and I decided that if Jay commented on it, I would say something like, "Hey, it's Canadian Club, not my fault," but he didn't say anything. When I turned my head, he wasn't even looking at me, preoccupied with something on his phone. I took a few more sips, brute-forcing through the urge to wince until it dissipated.

Jay picked up his cup and took a large swig, choking a little, his features recoiling. "You should have told me this stuff sucked."

"Hey," I said, "it's Canadian Club. I thought you knew." I shrugged. Casual. I know what I'm talking about. I know whiskey.

"I can mix it if you want," he offered before taking another sip and once again wrinkling in disgust. "Yeah, I'll mix it." He got up from the couch. "Coke okay?"

"And ice?"

"Sure thing, babe."

Once he was out of the room, I realized I was still wearing my jacket. I got up to shrug it off and draped it over the arm of the couch.

Jay came back in and placed the drinks back on the table. When he sat down, he reached into the pocket of his hoodie and pulled out a Ziploc bag with two sizeable looking brownies in them.

"You want?" he asked, and I nodded. He pulled one of the brownies from the bag and handed it to me before devouring the other. I looked down at my own, trying to somehow gauge how high it would get me and how high I was looking to get. "Should I just have half or –?"

Jay shrugged.

"Just tell me." I was feeling kind of ambivalent and didn't feel like making decisions. I had to work the next day, but it's not like my job required much of me besides being present and conscious enough to type numbers into a computer. Besides, if I got too tired, Jay would be able to drive me home, or I could get an Uber or something. There was never a question of whether I would be stuck, whether I would have a bad time and have to figure everything out myself. All I had to worry about were my immediate needs.

It occurred to me I was having one of those moments my friends would have scoffed at; they would have said some uppity, chastising thing about how I was putting myself in danger and needed to take better care of myself, blah blah blah. I understood it on some level. It seemed almost utopian that this guy would be trustworthy, give me free edibles, take me to dinner, have me over to his place, and make sure I got home safe while I was blasted out of my mind—but that's how it had always worked with us. The possibility of him being weird with me just wasn't on the table. I was content to put myself in his hands.

"Whole thing," Jay said with this kind of mischievous look on his face. "Live a little."

I obeyed, stuffing the whole thing in my mouth. I'd come to appreciate how Jay's edibles went down smooth. It was strong, still, despite the addition of the Coke and ice, all of it playing well with the chocolate—this little accidental gourmet moment. I licked the crumbs and chocolate residue off the tips of my fingers, feeling like a hedonist. In the unfocused background of my vision, I saw Jay's lip twitch a little.

"So, what are you feeling tonight? Movie or music?" Jay asked. This was something I'd grown to like about him; he always had options.

"Music is okay. I don't know if I have the attention span to watch something."

"Yes ma'am, sounds good." I was always babe or ma'am with Jay. He would say it, and I wouldn't feel much—usually.

Jay squinted at the rows of tightly-packed vinyl records lining the walls before disappearing back down the narrow hallway into what was presumably his bedroom and returning with a record in his hand.

"Are you a PJ Harvey kind of girl?"

"I don't know," I said, having never heard of her.

He paused for a second, then grinned. "You're a PJ Harvey kind of girl."

I laughed kind of uneasily. Something about being a Kind Of Girl who does anything never sat right with me. It was the same kind of thing that happened with whiskey. Handling it made you some specific person; not handling it made you another specific person. You were damned if you did, or if not, always torn between two different ideas, the distinctions so arbitrary. But I know Jay probably wasn't thinking in those terms, so I didn't say anything.

Jay played the record, and we sat there for a while in silence. I mean, not true silence since there was music, but we weren't talking, and this seemed significant. With other people, I may have felt the need to comment on the music, to give some indication I was enjoying this album I hadn't heard before. There was always that sense of being watched, an obligation to hold up my part of the deal by reacting. Much like many other things before it, I didn't realize how prominent this feeling usually was until I was with Jay and that feeling disappeared. And, once again, I wasn't sure what to do with such a revelation. The intro reached peak momentum, and PJ Harvey's vocals set in with this foreboding kind of discipline. You know there's more, and there will be more, but you aren't ready yet. PJ will get there when she gets there. And for now, this tease. She doesn't spare you any of the murk of it, dragging you behind her through the shroud she's creating. By the time she hits the first *to bring you, my love,* you're chest-deep, scared of where it's going but inexplicably needing to go there. She drops off, lets go, and for those few seconds, you dip down and become submerged completely. That's when you realize what all of the space in the song is: it's you. And by the time she comes back, it almost doesn't matter, because you've been under the surface, seen what's in that place, and you can't unsee it. And she's laying it on thicker now, crunchier. She's showing more of her cards or maybe gets you to show yours.

Later, you'll look up the lyrics to the song online and see all sorts of comments speculating, misguidedly trying to stick pins in whatever she sounds so wrought with. You'll want to chime in and tell every single one of them off, let them know you know they haven't gone under, they haven't been inside the spaces, not like you. Once you've been inside them, there's no way to talk about it. There's just the world, the song, the hole that's been chewed out of it, and if you're brave you can dangle your legs on the edge over the swirling grey pool and feel what you feel. But you'll know how insane that would sound to tell a stranger, so you'll give up and go on quietly changed.

The first track faded out, and whatever murk had filled the room began to retreat as if sucked up by some kind of unseen force and held there, waiting, against the walls. In its absence, becoming once again aware of the details of the room, I had this sensation of stepping out of a car after an hours-long drive, that five-minute crash course in walking you give yourself on the way to the gas station bathroom, thinking *Oh, it's late afternoon now. Oh,*

I crossed state lines, and it's warmer than I expected. You look in the smudged mirror for some kind of context and figure from your face that you're tired.

"Whoa," I said.

"Right?" Jay said. I had turned to look at him, only to find that he had already turned his focus to me and was awaiting my reaction. "And that's just the one song."

"That was crazy," I said. The next song had begun to play, and I'd lost the attention span to search for more interesting words.

This second song was chugging along, this low rumble, but I was still stuck in the first one. I was still trying to make sense of what had happened. The album's sleeve was propped up on one of the shelves, the cover in full view. A woman, PJ Harvey maybe, floating on her back in blue-grey water, dark hair trailing behind her, the ends dipping below the surface. If the album art was any indication, I'd had the intended experience.

Jay was working on his drink—real labor, it seemed—and he was absorbed, holding the Styrofoam cup up to his lips and chipping away with small slurps at the remaining liquid, pausing in between and cringing. I watched, though watching him seemed voyeuristic. I felt like a gender-reversal of some male-gazey movie, peering through some slit in a curtain as Jay did what he did, or what I imagined men like Jay did when they were alone. Drinking, listening to PJ Harvey with a serious pout—it was the male equivalent of brushing his long, flaxen hair in the mirror. You know, seated at a vanity by candlelight and sighing daintily at his reflection, unaware of the protagonist standing there, titillated, in the background. The protagonist feels vindicated in his inkling that this is a person worth wanting. And the audience agrees, and the person manning the camera agrees, and even if you don't agree you come away feeling sure that this is what it means to be beautiful. Watching Jay sip his drink that night, I can't say I didn't feel it. I can't say I did, but I also can't say that I didn't.

"I went on this spontaneous road trip one time," said Jay out of nowhere.

He belched quietly and placed his empty cup on the table, and I realized in the same moment that the second track had transitioned into the third. As if his action of putting down his cup, opening his mouth, and belching had somehow changed the entire mood of the room.

"I was trying to surprise this girl. She lived in Toledo; she was in college. And I wasn't really doing anything, so I threw a bunch of my shit in the car and thought I would just show up at her house and live there. Stopped at a rest stop about an hour away to let her know what I was doing, and she broke up with me there and then. I was standing at the payphone."

"Fuck."

"Yeah. I just drove the whole way back. I didn't have the apartment anymore, so I had to move back in with my folks. You know, tail between my legs," he laughed, picking up the cup to take another swig before realizing it was empty and setting it back down. "But I listened to this album on the way back. Just kept repeating it. It does something."

"Yeah, no, I know."

"I don't know what it does. I don't know if there's a way to talk about it. But there's—"

"Yeah."

"I knew you'd get it."

I ran a hand through my hair and shook it out to ground myself. "Did you guys ever talk again?"

"That girl?" He laughed in a way that seemed like it wasn't just at himself but also me. "No. I don't think we ever really talked after that. The whole thing was stupid. I was so young, you know?"

"I mean, sure."

"We were both trying to be too much for each other. It was for three years. You become your own little tribe after a while, or country; there's even a language. It's too much for one person."

"Isn't that the point, though? Like..." I paused to collect my thoughts, but it was already too late. I was trying desperately not to sound 22 and failing at it. "...finding someone?"

"Yeah, but she was trying to move in a different direction. We were too young for it. I might still be too young for it." He laughed weakly, and I followed suit. "I was 23. I couldn't be a partner to anyone. I mean, you know."

There it was. I was feeling something: a twinge. Something had collapsed or degraded, and suddenly I felt small and jealous, and suddenly my date of birth was tattooed in large print on my forehead. I managed a vague shrug of agreement and asked, "Where's the bathroom?" I couldn't tell Jay about the twinge because that's exactly what a naïve, underdeveloped 22-year-old would do. Maybe not the telling him about it but the feeling it in the first place, the taking it so personally. He gestured out of the doorway to another at the very end of the hall, looking concerned, but not overly so. I took another gulp of my drink and was halfway down the hallway by the time I swallowed it. Behind me, PJ Harvey was singing in a harsh whisper, and behind her, the bass rumbled like something hovering and preparing to touch down on the roof of Jay's building. *I'm just working / for the man / I'm just doing / what I can.*

The door separating the bathroom from the rest of the apartment was not a door but a long curtain, which wasn't a curtain but a long, itchy-looking blanket with a faded blue and orange Aztec-style pattern. It was heavy enough that, in a normal state, it would have felt like enough privacy. But in this particular moment, it felt like the punchline to a cruel joke being played on me by the universe: *You've just shown all your cards, now go take a piss in full view of the 45-year-old dude you've just shown all your cards to.* I looked in the mirror. The words *22-YEAR-OLD BABY* were scrolling above my head in neon red lettering. My thoughts were disorganized. I can't say how I felt exactly. Betrayed, maybe, in Jay's revelation of a distinction that had always existed between us but that I'd figured we'd silently agreed not to mention. Why did we have to draw attention to it? Why ruin a good thing?

I sat on the toilet for a few extra minutes, cycling through various apps on my phone. But I started to worry that I was being suspicious, that I had been in there too long and when I walked out Jay would make the honest mistake of asking me if I was okay, and then I'd have to tell him. Before opening the curtain, I pushed my hair back, adjusted my clothes—all of these little inconsequential movements to look less disheveled and more in charge of myself. It's silly in retrospect, trying to describe the motivation behind it. Like Jay would notice that my shirt was tucked in and my hair was out of my face and think, *Hey, that's a real adult woman, a person who has it together.* But I suppose that's what I thought.

When I walked out of the bathroom, the first room on the right had a light on, and Jay was standing there in front of the fridge, adding ice to our drinks.

"Hey," I said.

"Hey," Jay replied into the fridge, not looking at me, pulling out the two-liter of Coke he'd poured us before. "I was just re-upping the drinks." I nodded but didn't say anything, and he turned around, looking nervous. "I'm assuming you want to stay?"

"Yeah," I answered quickly, not thinking about it. There was a lot behind his question but I didn't know the contents exactly and wasn't interested in feeling them out. "It's only, like, 9:30, right?" My throat was dry.

"Yeah, plenty of time." He added Coke to one of the cups and then handed it to me. "I'll take you home whenever. Just give me a couple of hours' notice so I'm not stupid." He gestured to the bottle of whiskey on the counter.

I nodded. "Thank you." I could tell he was trying to find my eyes, but I continued staring at the cup. His eyes were too risky; too much had already happened.

"Anytime, babe."

That one, I felt.

Back on the couch, PJ Harvey had moved on from her reigned-in half-whisper, her drawl now low and nasty. Jay sat down next to me, roughly the same distance away, but it seemed more deliberate this time. I could see the line drawn on the couch cushion beside me. We sipped our drinks as the song droned and settled around us. Neither of us was talking. I turned to watch him, but there was something new there—an ache—and I felt marooned. The comfort from before was soiled or missing, and I found myself sitting in a dingy living room with someone who was less a friend and more a friendly stranger, sinking quickly into a mounting edible high that made it all that much heavier and harder to parse out.

"Okay," he said after some time, "what is it?"

"Nothing. Tired," I responded in a tone that neither of us felt particularly inclined to believe.

"You sure about that?"

My throat was drying up again. I held up my cup and drank, placing a particular focus on the rim of the cup, something to look at. It's not that I was being evasive on purpose, but I knew that the most truthful answer wouldn't come easily or quickly, and I wasn't sure I felt safe enough, and I wasn't sure I had the patience or the language.

Jay persisted. "Does this have anything to do with that night at the park?"

"What do you mean?"

"Come on."

"No, I don't know what you're talking about."

"You asked me if I thought of you as a kid."

"I definitely would remember asking that. I didn't ask that."

"You either asked it or you mentioned it. Something about how I thought of you as a kid. It was just something you said." PJ Harvey had finished singing, and the song wrapped up the first side of the album, leaving Jay and I suspended in midair. "And actually, I guess it couldn't have been a question because you didn't give me any time to answer it."

"Answer it then."

"How much do you want me to say? I don't think of you as a kid."

I didn't respond. It wasn't that I didn't believe his answer. I couldn't decide if I was satisfied with it.

"You're my friend. Sometimes the younger thing comes up, but I don't know."

Jay touched his chin, dug the back of his nail into the stubble under his bottom lip. I got the sense that he was trying to choose his words carefully, to find the right way of saying the kind of thing likely to be taken in a thousand other less-delicate ways. "But I don't feel *weird* about it. It's all good here if it's all good with you. Is that what you were looking for?"

"Yeah," I said, and then, "I don't know."

Jay pressed his lips together into a flat line and turned toward me like he was trying to stare into my face, through it rather than at it, like there was some question left hanging open, something I was hesitating to surrender. But if there was, I didn't know it, or I couldn't reach far enough to get it. It wasn't coming out tonight in his apartment in this whiskey/brownie fog. He held this stare for a few seconds, but it wasn't long before the silence began to get to him, too, and he got up to flip the record.

"Wait," I said. "I'm not really feeling like music anymore."

"Fair enough, babe." He stopped and turned around to look at me. "Watch something?"

"Yeah," I said.

Jay sat back down on the couch next to me, reached for the laptop on the table, and pulled it toward us. While it was booting up, he said, "I don't have Netflix Instant on this thing yet, so..." and gestured to the TV a few feet away.

"Oh?" It took me a few seconds to realize what he was talking about. Netflix Instant is what they called the thing we now understand as just normal Netflix back when Netflix didn't deal almost exclusively in streaming content and still mailed people DVDs. I thought briefly about making fun of him for this, of asking him whether Netflix still sent him DVDs in the mail, but I hesitated. We'd already drawn enough attention to the age difference for one night, and hopefully for more than one night.

We decided on *Stargate SG-1*. It was one of the few pieces of media Jay and I seemed to have in common, and it seemed like the kind of content a cool adult person (to Jay) might decide to watch while stoned. There wasn't much deliberation regarding what season to watch—the mounting body load from the brownies made it difficult to make decisions and unlikely either of us would be able to follow the plot at all anyway. Jay loaded up some random episode, and we sunk into the couch, his thigh against my thigh. There was little talking. Every few minutes my hearing would slip out of phase, and I would no longer be able to parse what the characters were saying. There would only be the stagnant fuzziness of the room and the hum of the refrigerator down the hall and the cicadas outside, and I would think to myself that I was somehow achieving tranquility, that I was emptying my mind. Then one of the characters in *Stargate SG-1* would say something, and it would be like they yanked me back to the couch with one of those Vaudeville hooks. Sure, kid. Serenity. If you say so. Don't quit your day job.

It was one of the earlier episodes—the one where Samantha Carter is captured by a member of an alien tribe who hopes to exchange her for the daughter of an enemy chief. This particular tribe mandates that women are forbidden from speaking or appearing in public under the penalty of death. The other members of SG-1 attempt to rescue Carter, but it's ultimately her tenacity that allows her to secure her freedom. I had a vague memory of watching the episode a few years prior and feeling deeply disturbed by it. But tonight, I felt none of those things. I had no connection to the people moving around on the screen. They were minding their own business, and I followed suit.

"I always thought Carter was kind of hot," I said, just to say something. Well, not really just to say something. It was the whiskey thing again. Whether I found Samantha Carter on *Stargate SG-1* especially attractive was irrelevant, was a fact hidden even from me amidst all of the obvious signalings. *I know women, I know hot women, and I can be bawdy about it, too, aren't I such a spitfire?*

"Yeah?"

"Yeah. She's, like, tough."

Jay looked at me and then at the laptop. "I guess."

"You don't agree!"

"I don't know. Not my type, I guess."

"No taste," I teased.

"I have taste!" Jay said. "I just don't really do the short hair thing."

"Then you definitely don't have taste."

Jay shrugged.

"I would do her," I added, Just To Say Something.

"Oh yeah?" Jay touched the side of my foot with his own. A flash, but there were flashes everywhere now, something I pretended not to notice as I kept my eyes locked onto the screen.

"Yeah."

"Good for you. Like I said, not my type."

"Oh, come on," said the girl. I didn't remember how I'd gotten up there, but I was clinging, now, to the drop ceiling, watching the girl below me shift in her seat and swallow hard. "You would still watch," she said.

"I would," said Jay.

The girl gulped again. Her eyes hadn't moved from the screen, but it was clear the show had zero holds on her attention. Her socked foot slid up the back of Jay's ankle, and Jay breathed hard. The girl looked at him and saw his mouth was half-open, saw where his eyes were.

There's this trope that's common in movies where the two characters who were going to end up together from the beginning, who were destined and scripted to kiss, finally do it, and it happens like a lunge. The self-control molts away and leaves behind two horny lizard brains, and they come swinging and slopping into each other like slabs of defenseless pink meat. I want you to know that this isn't what happened between Jay and the girl in his apartment. There was no feeling of finality, no immediate release. The girl was uncertain, and the man next to her was even more so, and when they disconnected from each other's lips, they shared a look of bewilderment and horror. The girl pivoted on the couch so that she was perpendicular to the man, and she folded her legs so she was sitting on her heels. The girl touched the man's shoulder, and he kissed her again, and this time she bit his lip, and this time he placed his hand on the back of her neck, and this time it lasted longer, and when they pulled away from each other their breaths were mangled with the inhales omitted. The man laid back on the couch, and the girl hovered over him, and they kissed again—this time multiple times in a row, this time with her opening her mouth to let in the man's tongue which felt foreign and strangely dry.

And the girl indeed made a sound I won't repeat here. And she indeed slid her hand under the man's shirt, and she rubbed her palm on the soft, dark hair clustered above the waistband of his jeans, and noted it, and lingered there. But none of it was fluid. There were none of these long, winding sentences. From the ceiling, I could see all of the cracks in what looked like pure instinct, how every clumsy moment was a kind of bargaining, a way to paint over the obvious questions. They kept unfolding one after the other, these tacit agreements to procrastinate, give the id ten more seconds to fill up its pockets. And it was only when the man groaned—a deep and reckless growl that drew immediate attention to both his roughness and his age—that the girl on top of him flinched and rushed to the far end of the couch. And when they looked at each other, breaths still ragged, there was no pink meat, just some man and some girl left to answer for the preceding moment and its many debts.

When I blinked, I was no longer on the ceiling. I was sitting up against the arm of the couch with my knees folded up to my chest and my hair falling into my face. I was wet, and my breaths were ragged. I wanted to ask what the fuck had happened, but it seemed like an unfair question. We had both been there; we had both received the same information. Jay was a few feet away, his limbs pulled deliberately close. He was fiddling with the collar of his shirt.

"Sorry," he said.

"You don't have to say that."

We caught our breaths, and then Jay said, "I can take you home."

"Okay," I said. I rushed off to the bathroom. I cupped my hands and ran them under the faucet and drank. When I picked my head up, I caught my reflection in the mirror. The girl's shirt was untucked. Her hair was flying out in all directions. And I wasn't staring down at her from the ceiling, even though I wanted to be.

When I returned to the living room, Jay was missing, and his bedroom door was closed. I gathered up my wallet and jacket and balled both up under my arm. The laptop was still on, still playing *Stargate SG-1*. O'Neill and Teal'c were facing off with the alien tribe, and O'Neill was trying to intimidate one of the men by showing off his firepower. He was shooting a gun at the wall, and the tribesmen were startled. Somewhere outside our field of view, Samantha Carter was trying to blend in among the other women to survive. Or maybe she was talking to one of the other tribesmen, having her kind of confrontation. Either way, the characters on the show didn't comprehend what had just happened between Jay and me in his apartment. They hadn't been paying attention to us. As I stood in front of the couch adjusting my shirt, it occurred to me that, if we'd let the music on, maybe things would have played out a bit differently. PJ Harvey would have paid attention. She wouldn't have let Jay be so apologetic and offer to drive me home or let me be so quick to oblige. She would have floated over and dunked our heads under the water and forced us to acknowledge what had just happened.

Jay stepped out of his room wearing a hoodie and said, "Are you ready?"

I nodded.

The cat, Patti Smith, was napping at the top of the stairs. I followed Jay's lead in stepping over her as we both made our way out of the apartment and back into his car. The ten-minute ride back to my building was silent. I spent most of it staring out the window, staring at the other cars. I imagined, as I often did when I was sad, that the other cars were occupied by normal people who had normal relationships with each other and were making trips for normal reasons: picking their daughters up from friends' houses; running out to grab some milk for tomorrow's coffee. Whenever I did look over at Jay, he turned away as if he'd been staring, too. I was trying to pretend the warmth that I felt was the only embarrassment, that I kept replaying the tape of us in my head out of shame only. I was telling myself, *You can imagine it all you want for now, but once you leave the car, you have to forget any of this ever happened.* Eventually, he pulled up in front of my building, and I didn't even let the car stop completely before opening the door and beginning to climb out.

"Wait," he said. I had to hold my hand in front of my face to keep my heart in my mouth.

I turned back around with one leg hanging out of the car. Our eyes found each other for half a second before it became too much and we pointed them elsewhere.

"Just your food," Jay said, gesturing at the Styrofoam container on the floor in front of my seat.

I reached down to grab it, and then leaped out of the car completely, leaning on my left leg. "Thanks."

"Yup."

"Thank you for the ride."

Jay nodded. I shut the door, and he pulled away from the curb.

Standing in the elevator with my cold container of linguini in my hand, I tried to stop playing the tape but couldn't. I was cold and drunk and stoned and it seemed within the realm of possibility that I would have to spend the rest of my life this way, hearing Jay say, "I would," over and over, his thick tongue bursting through the left wall of my every thought and feeling. It was "The Tell-Tale Heart," pink meat under all of the floorboards.

When I got inside, I ripped off my jeans and ate the linguini straight from the box, pawing through my phone with my other hand, desperate for something not-Jay, not-tongue, not-meat to occupy me or steal my attention.

On Facebook, it said that Sidney and Ant were finally, officially, In A Relationship. The congratulations that were certainly in order felt to me like the perfect diversion.

I called her twice, but she didn't pick up.

WORK

I called off work the next day because I couldn't think. I had dinner plans with Sidney which I kept. I couldn't let her know what happened at Jay's the night before or that I now felt unknown to myself, too frantic to type numbers into an Excel sheet for eight hours. I told her to pick me up at the office and walked the whole way there to sell my lie. When she showed up, I was sitting on the curb with my chin in my palm, scrolling through my phone, sighing like I'd downloaded some looping animation of a Woman Who'd Worked All Day.

Sidney's car pulled up to the curb, and I rushed inside. When I shut the passenger-side door, something lifted. Sitting on the curb, I had accumulated this weight, having to consider how weird I did or didn't look at other people walking on the street. I was convinced anyone who looked at me could immediately tell Something Had Happened. But in Sidney's car, I was protected, absolved of any need to perform. Well, except for the fact that I was reeling over what happened at Jay's—a fact which I felt I could not tell her under any circumstances.

"Hey," she said.

"Hey."

I kept my head turned toward the window, afraid that looking directly at the face of someone who knew me would shatter the veil of carefully-practiced nonchalance that had, until now, kept me from bursting into tears. "Work sucked," I added, continuing my performance of the Woman Who'd Worked All Day.

"Yeah, seriously," she said. "They told me today they 'don't have any more assignments.' I worked too fast. There's nothing."

"So, what's gonna happen?"

Somehow, I knew next to nothing about what Sidney did for a living. It was some kind of web thing or copywriting. She had a contract for the next few months with some vague possibility for them to hire her again, maybe permanently. Though from what she had just said, that possibility was no longer a serious one. None of this was surprising. It was the ultimate fate of nearly all contract jobs. Two or three months of poorly-paid work, of sitting in the shittiest desk in the darkest corner of the office, some flimsy suggestion of full-time or benefits that dries up as soon as you get comfortable enough to plan. It was either that or working 29 hours a week at some equally shitty place that deliberately keeps you too busy to get a second job and just below the threshold to entitle you to healthcare. I knew of a lot of other people in Sidney's position, hopping from contract to contract, chasing the scent of full-time prospects. Modern job searching was a lot like modern dating, except with life-or-death consequences and somehow even more rampant commitment-phobia. I was lucky. I didn't know anyone else my age with a permanent full-time job.

"They have to keep me for a few months still," Sidney said. "So now it's just bullshit. I dunno."

"Well, at least you still get paid right? It buys you some time at least?"

Sidney snorted. "Yeah, I mean, sure." I was still looking out the window, but I could feel her rolling her eyes nonetheless. "They told me to wear 'comfortable clothes' when I come in next week. They're going to have me clean the bathrooms. So that's cool."

"Fuck," I said.

"No, it's okay, I guess," Sidney said. "I mean hands-on stuff can be good, right? I'm paid the same."

"And it's not forever," I added.

"Yeah, exactly. It's not forever."

I was quiet for a while, chain-swallowing anxieties as Sidney drove. When I turned, I noticed this new look on her face—this lightness—and I envied it: the way she looked somehow unbothered, even in the throes of professional uncertainty and burnout. Like something had been out of place all this time—this small, stubborn knot that, for the first time in her entire life, had loosened, and now nothing could exhaust her. And even though I should have been happy for her, it was mostly bitterness that I felt. Sidney was supposed to be the person who could never figure it out. Her back-and-forth with Ant had become its own kind of natural law, the rhythm by which everything else in my world could be rationalized and understood. As long as it was there, we could all coast awhile—a running gag that made us characters in some episodic show with no real arcs and no responsibility to invest in our lives. Sidney and Ant committing to each other had destroyed this illusion of timelessness. And as she took us onto I-79 toward the South Side I could feel it all crumbling around me. I went white there in the passenger seat, sweating beneath a mound of existential problems I now felt there was no time left to solve.

We went back to the burger place. We both had long days, though in my case for reasons I kept hidden, and it seemed like too much work to make any additional decisions about where to go. Sidney got us a pitcher of beer and we sat quietly, puzzling over our order sheets. It occurred to me then that choosing this place to avoid decision-making was misguided. The idea that I had to select a winning combination of burger toppings in this state seemed cruel. I checked off exactly what I had gotten the last time. When the waiter came around to collect our orders I wouldn't look at him, suddenly reminded of all the times I turned in a half-assed assignment at school, dreading the grade

When he walked away, I took a long draw of my beer and said, "So. Ant, huh?"

The grin that spread across her face indicated she'd been waiting for me to ask. "Yeah. I don't know, it was weird."

"In what way?"

"He's the one who brought it up. I was afraid to do it this time. Like, things were going well, and the last thing I wanted to do was be like, 'Let's actually be together, let's go through that whole bullshit again.' So, I wasn't going to say anything, and then he randomly was like, 'I want us to be exclusive. I feel like things are serious,' and obviously, I agreed. It was weirdly simple."

"He said that?"

"Not exactly that, but yeah. We were in bed, and I watched him set up the Facebook thing. It was nice."

"Well, I'm glad that finally happened. I can't say I expected that."

She snorted. "Yeah, I mean, me neither. But I should have known it was going to happen like this." Buzzing and manic in a way that seemed to differ from her usual, she had already finished her first beer and began refilling her glass from the pitcher between us. "Like, after I had given up on it happening ever." There was a tinge of exasperation in her words, albeit a playful one.

"It didn't really seem like you gave up, though," I said.

"Well, I didn't, but you know. I was doing my own thing for a while. Not waiting for him necessarily, but waiting."

"At the fountain," I blurted.

"What?"

"Nevermind."

Sidney was quiet for a moment. Then she said, "So, we're moving in together."

I almost choked on my beer. "Yeah?"

"Yeah." She grinned down at her glass. "His house is like, nice. Like, it looks like a real adult home."

"Yeah?"

"Yeah. Like, I know it sounds stupid, but his posters are *framed*. And he has a whole extra bedroom for me to keep all of my bullshit. So, I'm moving in next month."

I thought about Jay's apartment—the dark carpets with Patti Smith's fur baked in. The smell of the lemon air freshener and pot; the scratchy couch with its torn upholstery; the texture of his beard. Just for a moment, before I could yank the leash away from the forbidden territory. Were there posters, and were they framed? I pictured that living room, the walls bloated with media. No room in his bedroom, either, I assumed, given that he seemed to be using it to store the overflow of his record collection. And on that note, the notion of a spare bedroom was also laughable.

I considered what it would be like to tell Sidney everything. To listen to Sidney tell me about her future Real Adult Home and then let her know I made out with a 45-year-old Dusty Apartment Guy. That I had run my finger enticingly along the waistband of a man in his 40's whose bathroom door was a blanket. A new, more confusing level of sickness washed over me, and, in its wake, made my lust all the more humiliating. But what would Jay have to say about any of this? He probably never noticed this sort of thing. He was on his path, one where functioning bathroom doors and age-appropriate décor were not massive priorities. That was what I liked about him. He had seen the life that was ahead of him—the normal job and the Real Adult Apartment— and decided he didn't want any of it. He didn't worry about looking like a Real Adult, and I shouldn't, either. And yet.

"The other day we were talking about logistical stuff, like, when I would show up and how we would move stuff out of my place." In the span of a moment I realized Sidney was still talking, and I had been that horrible person who glazes over while their friends are trying to celebrate their successes. "I asked him what day would be best to do the bulk of the moving, and he pulled out his phone calendar. I just felt like that was so adult."

"Yeah, that bodes well, I think."

"Are you good?" Sidney asked. She'd seen through my half-assed attempt at conversation and was now trying to meet my eyes over our near-empty pitcher of Blue Moon.

I nodded, shrugged. "Yeah, sorry. I was up really late so I just kind of feel like—" I stuck out part of my tongue, letting my chin drop.

Sidney made an *mm* sound mid-swallow and then said, "Didn't you go out with Jay last night?"

"Yeah, he dropped me off late." I looked over my shoulder at nothing. Casual.

"What did you guys do?"

"We just got some food and smoked had a little bit to drink."

It was a normal question, at least in the context of the limited information Sidney had been given, but I was sweating. I knew transparency wasn't an option. Even if I wanted to tell her the full story, I wouldn't know how to explain it. The chronology was still hazy and hard to pin down, and maybe that was how I preferred it. But the weight of the full truth was still immense. I felt it wafting up from under my feet, the stench of pink meat gone off. Maybe I could appease us both with a fraction of the truth, eat around the edge of it. "I feel like I drank too much. I woke up, and I felt like shit."

Sidney nodded, satisfied if not totally convinced. "Beer will help," she said, sliding the pitcher in my direction. "You can finish it off."

I did as I was told, topping off my nearly-empty glass with the last of our communal beer. When I finished pouring, I lifted it and took a long swig that did nothing for the knot in my stomach but gave me something to do while being watched.

The rest of the evening went by rather uneventfully. The brief intermission for my angst ended, and Sidney continued filling me in on her newly-committed relationship with Ant. I tried my best to seem, at worst, bored instead of shaken and bitter. I'd already heard most of it before in the days preceding some of their earlier near-misses, where Sidney and I would sit in a restaurant, not unlike this one after work, and she would gush to me about how much Ant had changed and how much he impressed her and how great he was in bed. Only this time her statements were weighted. I could even see it in the way her hands moved as she spoke, this certainty that she was loved. It might be that I'd never had that same glow about me, and the possibility was frightening. Equally as frightening was the possibility that I had it right then, that I was sitting across from her, oozing it, and she knew why.

The waiter made his way over to the table with our burgers. Sidney had been more adventurous than last time and was presented with a stack of muddied toppings half-slumped over onto the far side of the plate, a situation that the waiter excitedly deemed A Knife-and-Fork-er. I felt relieved to have stayed within my comfort zone, but when I bit into my burger it wasn't like before. It tasted like plastic. I looked around at the restaurant, its dark, heavy tables stained and deliberately nicked to look rustic. A waitress walked by holding a pair of drinks served in mason jars. We were sitting in an anachronistic, high-budget Hollywood set version of an old saloon, LARPing as burger connoisseurs.

I couldn't help but remember what Jay said about finding good food in restaurants. How you had to find the most run-down hole-in-the-wall place to eat a real meal. I bit into my plastic avocado burger and considered the possibility that he was right. But, as always, there was that persistent denial, the aversion I always felt to this sort of thing—to be the kind of person who had rules about what kind of restaurants served Real Food. I always believed that, at some point, resisting the elite makes you an elitist, but I could feel the things Jay said beginning to poison me. But it couldn't be denied. I went to the bathroom before we left, and the floors were shiny, and there was no writing on the stalls, and it was fully stocked with soap and paper towels. In the spotless mirror, I thought to myself, *Of course,* and then, *You fucking traitor.*

Sidney and I split up right after dinner. She had a movie night with Ant and I had some lie about needing Pedialyte and sleep. When I got back to my apartment, I read my emails. It was the first time I'd checked them all day, scared that I'd hear from Jay before I was ready and phase fully out of reality. Sandwiched between coupons and marketing emails for self-proclaimed lifestyle gurus who had collected me over the years was an email from one of my supervisors telling me to get well soon. Below that, I found it: the inevitable email from Jay with the subject line: *when youre ready.*

THE EMAIL

The email was three paragraphs long and began with an unnecessarily self-flagellating apology. He said he was sorry that he Made Things Weird and he understood if I Felt Too Uncomfortable to Continue. He wanted to let me know that he meant what he said before: that he didn't think of me as a kid, that he didn't intend for Things Between Us to go That Way. But in all of those paragraphs, there was no real specificity. I didn't learn any of the information I'd been hoping for; there were no definitions. What were the Things he made weird? What were Things Between Us? What way was That Way? It was the same problem that caused all of this, that allowed me to end up straddling him at 10 PM on the couch in his apartment. Just like when it happened, I didn't need the apology, which was just some reinforcement of the 22-year-old girl/45-year-old man thing I thought we'd already hashed out. I wanted to know what he did after he dropped me off that night. I wanted to know if he, too, had fallen asleep with the last few lines of our conversation looping in his head, haunted by the phantom sensation of his tongue in my mouth.

The meat of the email, after the pained introduction, was an invitation. He wanted to pick me up again sometime soon—go have a drink and talk things out. *When I was ready*, it said. That part was key. He was making space for some future version of me who knew how I felt and what I wanted, specifically and without any of his input. I wasn't sure that version of myself as possible. But I was more curious about his feelings than my own. I struggled to imagine myself going another few days, let alone a week, without knowing them.

To make the email happen, I flipped a switch. walked out and made the girl left behind get the words on the screen. She had this sense of duty that I trusted. She did the things that needed to be done. Her fingers moved, and I watched her pacing.

Hey, she typed. *You don't have to say sorry, but thanks. We can meet tomorrow if you want. You can pick me up after work, usual spot.*

Satisfied with the content of the message, I tried to run back to the girl, trying to hit Send for her before she could do any additional damage. But when I got up to rush toward her, I realized I'd been sitting on the edge of my bed the entire time, the exact spot where she'd been standing.

I hit Enter a few times and then, to my horror, added a sentence to the closing of the email: *I know things are going to be weird but I want you to know I thought it was nice.*

Those words haunted me all the next day, bouncing off the walls of my otherwise-empty skull as I embarked upon an ill-advised first day back at work. It turned out that even data entry was nearly impossible when you felt this bad. I cut out early to try and fix myself up in the office bathroom. I felt like my face was covered in slime. I took a few brown paper towels from the dispenser and blotted my nose and cheeks, gave myself the real Slice of Pizza treatment. I'd always felt that the specific type of brown paper towel available in public bathrooms was especially adept at absorbing grease like they were made from some impossible high-tech synthetic material, one originally developed by the DoD for some nefarious purpose, or for controlling oil spills, and then had unwittingly made it into the hands of the public. After examining my newly-mattified face in the mirror, I combed my fingers through my hair. I couldn't believe I was doing this again, pushing my hair out of my face, straightening my shirt for him, trying to look adult and impressive. I considered briefly that, after the events of the other night, he would most likely not be swayed in either direction by my French tuck, but that was a thought that led quite easily to other less-than-ideal thoughts, and we weren't going to think about those. We weren't going there. It simply couldn't be done.

In the email, I'd said to meet at the usual spot, so Jay picked me up down the road from work. All of these evenings getting dinner with him, and he never figured out where the front door of my office was. He probably didn't know where I worked. I appreciated this, relished in it. At this point, I was grasping for whatever minor air of mystery I could manage to achieve. Jay's AC had already ruined my hair. I tried to reconfigure my part by feel as Jay started the car and pulled away from the curb.

"Hey."

I was grateful he'd spoken first. "Hi," I said. I didn't look at him.

"You look good."

I buried a smile. "Thanks. I look like shit right now, though."

"Oh, come on." I let my eyes meet him just in time to see them roll in playful exasperation. "You never look like shit."

"You come on!" I shot back. It felt nice to be doing our usual thing, bantering, playing hot potato with a simple compliment. As I laughed, I shifted, and my left arm briefly brushed his right, sending a thick ring of heat pulsing outward from the spot where we touched. There was less tension than there should have been between us, all things considered. Just the same flashes as before, now accompanied by the knowledge of what exactly was behind them.

When we both cooled down, Jay said, "So, I thought we could go somewhere, get a drink."

"Yeah, that's fine," I said.

We didn't talk much during the drive, much like most of our drives. But unlike the rest of our drives, Jay hadn't put on any music, leaving few neutral points of entry should either of us have felt like putting an end to the silence. There was, of course, the obvious, but I had the sense that neither he nor I was ready to have that conversation. We were on our way to spend the evening in a public place, one where we would be served alcoholic beverages, and there was a reason for that choice of venue.

I listened to the air rushing through the vents as Jay drove. Even with my poor sense of direction, I recognized the route we were on. We'd gone this way before. It was easy to ignore at first; it was just a road. Plenty of people drive down these roads every day feeling any number of feelings. Then I would see a building or a light in the distance or some particular section of guardrail that I recognized and feel there again. Back inside those stretched-out minutes spent blinking slowly at my drunk reflection in the window, wrestling the ghost of his tongue. I looked over at Jay, trying to scan his face for his version of those old feelings. He was locked onto the road in front of him, radiating heat. I would have sworn I saw the space around him warping and twisting, like the air above a lit grill. Those wet, sad eyes.

He took us to this little pub in his neighborhood. Though I was sweating from nerves, I wished I'd worn a jacket. We were in that transition period leading into fall where the evenings were much cooler than the days. By the end of the day, you were unseasonable, and there was nothing you could do to avoid it. I tensed up, trying not to shiver when the air hit me. I got that creeping dread of having brushed off your mother's insistence you bring a jacket to school only to realize that she had been right—why does that particular feeling stick with you forever? It was the last thing I needed at this moment when I was trying to be an equal, an Adult. In a rush, I set off across the road too early, only to be pulled back toward the curb by one of Jay's arms. A pulse of heat ran through me as a car sped past less than a foot from where I was standing, its driver leaning on the horn. Jay cupped his whole hand around one of my forearms and hissed at the cold.

"Damn," he said. "I have a jacket back in the car if you want it?"

"Nah, we'll be inside anyway." I winced internally. I could feel my hair getting more windblown by the second.

"Okay, if you're sure."

"Yeah."

Jay held the door open for me as we entered. The pub was fairly empty—one could assume the people in this neighborhood did not, for whatever reason, do happy hour. Jay and I made our way to a booth across from the bar, and I felt the few other patrons spinning in their stools to stare at us as we moved past. I felt them being acutely aware of us and our mismatched-ness and our ages, and I felt them being acutely aware of my awareness of them. Or at least I imagined I did. There was a jukebox in the corner—one of those digital ones where you could pay to queue up whatever songs you wanted—playing "We Are the Champions." I still felt cold.

When we sat down, Jay lightly slapped his palms on the table in front of us and said, "So, what am I getting you?"

"Whatever you get," I said.

"You sure?"

"Yeah."

I watched him walk over to the bar, eavesdropped on his muffled order of two Yuenglings. He gestured back toward our table, and I winced. I was worried the bartender would ask for my card, and I would have to shuffle up there all pale and twiggy next to him, and everything would become weird. But all she did was nod and walk away to fill our glasses. This place *was* a few blocks from Jay's; maybe he knew her. Hanging above our table was this tacky light fixture: a yellowish dome with stained-glass parrots perched around the rim. I stared at it, waiting.

It wasn't long before Jay returned. He placed my glass in front of me. "I come here with Tom a lot."

"Yeah?"

"Yeah," Jay said. He took a long swig. "He lives around here, too. He'll just park at mine, we'll eat an edible, and then walk up. Those are some good nights."

I swallowed my sip of beer and felt my head immediately clouding. "Sounds like it," I said.

"Yeah."

We both took long drinks from our glasses. The jukebox had stopped playing Queen and was transitioning into "Wish You Were Here" by Pink Floyd. I looked up at the ceiling as it played.

"So," said Jay after a minute. "Look."

"Looking," I said.

"I just want to say again that it is not my intention to make you uncomfortable. I am totally fine with and appreciate our friendship." There it was, that same tone from the email again—the formulaic apology.

"Why are you doing that?" I asked.

"Doing what?" Jay sat back in his seat. He looked vaguely hurt by my question.

"Like, apologizing like that. Like I'm scared of you? We were friends, I thought. It's fine to just..." I took a drink to collect my thoughts. "It's fine to just say shit."

The silence that came after puzzled me. Maybe I'd been a little more forceful than usual, but I didn't think I'd exploded. Still, when I looked at Jay, I got the sense that something had shattered. He looked like a beaten dog. I know describing him this way presumes that someone had—metaphorically—just beaten him and that that person was me, but it was true. He picked up his glass but didn't drink from it, just stared down at the surface of his beer the way characters in movies gaze into bodies of water.

After a long sigh, he said, "I told Tom about us, or this."

"Okay?" I instantly began welling up with hot anger, if only because I'd taken such great pains to keep the events of the other night a secret. But I knew better than to lash out.

"Not the other night," he added. I felt the muscles in my back slacken. "But just that we've been spending time together. The general idea of it."

"Okay, so, what did he say?" I was getting impatient, I figured there was a roughly 40% chance that this conversation was ever going to go somewhere.

Jay sighed again. "He told me to be careful. Because—"

"Because I'm 22."

"Yeah."

"Jesus," I said, "it's not like I'm a baby."

"Yeah, I know that." Jay was the last patient he'd ever been in my presence, his lips stretched into a tense little strip. He inhaled slowly. "But you're also the one who asked me if I saw you as a kid."

"So?"

"So, you know, it's a delicate thing." Somehow, without realizing it, both of us had been gradually lowering our voices since Jay had returned to our booth, and he was leaning in towards me now with all of the hushed urgency of a criminal describing a heist. "Do you think you're the only one who feels confused by this? Seriously? After I dropped you off, I felt like the biggest creep on earth. I couldn't sleep. I was like, how am I this guy?"

"What? What guy?"

"I don't know!" Jay said. "The guy who, like, gets close to chicks half his age and then tries to sleep with them, or something. And gets them drunk in his apartment."

"How is that any better than getting me drunk in a cemetery?" I asked. "Or, like, the park? Or taking me to dinner two nights a week? All of which I agreed to, by the way."

"It's not, I guess. I just didn't think about it like that before. Like, as a pattern. Things were always weird, but I'm a weird person, so we went out and did weird shit together." For a minute, the friction gave way and he laughed a little. I tried to laugh, too, or at least meet his eyes. Something to diffuse the weird adversarial energy—*See? I'm here too, I'm also laughing, I have more agency than some paper-thin concept of a Younger Woman.* We spent a second in that weird liminal space, awkwardly chuckling. I took another sip of my beer, peered at him warmly—with a hint of mischief, even—over the rim of the glass. Then, the intermission ended, and Jay let out a long sigh. "I don't know. And then I ruined it by being the creepy old guy who tries to get you to stay over."

"What are you talking about? You drove me home. I didn't even say I wanted to leave. After we made out, the first thing you said was sorry. How is that creepy at all?"

"Okay, fine," said Jay, "but imagine if I didn't. "

"If you didn't? I don't know." I reached to break up the dialogue with a sip of beer, only to realize my glass was empty. "I guess I would have just kept going."

"Yeah?"

"Yeah." I looked at him, and the air between us sizzled. "But now you're doing this, like, weird thing where you just keep beating yourself up and apologizing as you threw yourself at me, and I have no fucking idea how you felt about it. You're trying to get out of my way, and it's weird."

Jay finished his beer, belched quietly. I could tell he was collecting his thoughts. On my end, things had become frustrating. I'd agreed to meet up with him in the hopes that I'd find some clarity or at least closure. Instead, I was giving a 45-year-old man a pep talk about how he wasn't creepy or taking advantage of me, all the while admitting to both him and myself that I found the events of the other night hot, actually, and would have kept going. There was no going back now. I was disarmed, exposed. What I wanted now was for him to give some indication he agreed.

Eventually, he said, "So what if I got out of your way?"

"I don't know."

"Sounds like you do."

I felt something touch my foot under the table, and my stomach lurched. When I looked up to meet Jay's eyes, what happened was beyond a flash.

I'D SHUDDER TOO

My first kiss was in eighth grade with this guy named Dalton who came to my best friend's birthday party, held me down, and stole a Starburst out of my mouth. Dalton was a little older than the rest of us. He was in high school, had apparently been an Abercrombie model, and wore entirely too much cologne. When our friends went upstairs to check on the birthday brownies, we stayed in the basement and made out on the musty hand-me-down couch. I experienced the kissing in third-person, editorializing the spectacle of his tongue forcing its way into my mouth, his cold hand clumsily snaking its way under the hem of my shirt. There was little attention paid to his skill in kissing, or lack thereof, or the number of bases the two of us may or may not be reaching together, the smacking of our lips veiled from the parents' awareness only by the hum of the chest freezer near the bottom of the stairs. The attraction was in the optics—the idea that I was kissing a sixteen-year-old boy in my best friend's basement. I was so young and innocent and weird; and he was older, mannish, with a coarse beginning of a beard sprouting in patches on his jaw. He was blonde, with these hard, blue eyes. When he pulled me against his chest, he prickled the hair on my arms with the icy-hot double-whammy of musk and peppermint. He told me I "kissed like a crack addict," and somehow, I took this to be a good thing. But mostly what I experienced was that he was older—the miracle of his attention, third-person awareness of lips on lips, and then his hand under my shirt, letting it happen.

It was like this now, too, in Jay's bedroom. I watched him kiss me through a haze of lemony disinfectant. I watched us claw at each other, stacks of books and records towering around us like stalagmites and my socks disappearing somewhere I'd never find them again. We'd come here straight from the bar, watched two minutes of a movie before somehow ending up in this room with the door closed, with the light still on. Below me, a young woman—a girl, got undressed and lay face-up and perfectly still, as if not a person.

"My roommate's home," said Jay, coming up from her neck for air.

The girl was shocked at the idea that this roommate had existed and made a mental note of it. But her face didn't betray any of these distractions, her eyes stony, aimed over his shoulder at the ceiling—at me.

He put his mouth close to her ear. "We have to be quiet."

The girl hummed, or maybe murmured something, or maybe just thought she did. After all, she had floated so far away from her body—not to be confused with escaping, detaching, fear. She wasn't afraid, not unwilling. Not in theory. She had, if she was being honest, imagined this before. The gruffness in his voice—he was so much more experienced, so much older, and yet capable, still, of feeling so much. And surely when he placed his hand on her, that immensity of feeling would vibrate through it and into her skin, a kind of certainty that this moment was, no pun intended, the climax of Something Important. Instead, there was just his hand on her, sliding its way up her stomach. His hand felt like it was made out of paper. When it began slightly broaching the underside of her breast, she flinched, and he flinched in response.

"Sorry," he said, his voice softening as he continued. "You're probably not used to that."

"What?" I was back in the bed now, firmly rooted in my body.

"You're probably not used to being touched like that by a man." He gazed down at her beneath a pair of perfectly-furrowed eyebrows, his tone strained and paternal.

"Oh," I said. I wasn't sure if he was referring to my recent breakup or our general age difference or just some perceived lack of experience on my part. "It's okay."

"Sorry," he said and then continued gazing for a moment as if satisfied by this momentary lapse and for having said the things he had.

Aside from the door theory, there was another thing about sex that I'd come to understand as universally true: when you were with someone, and there was chemistry, nothing could ever be awkward. Things could be funny, and they could be awkward in retrospect, but the whole thing could never come crashing down after a weird comment or a moment of incoordination. This once-airtight theory was now being called into question as I felt all of the heat in the room disperse and escape through the crack under the door.

I made no mention of this, just sunk back into the bed as Jay lunged back toward me with an urgency that had been building since Taco House, since that night at the cemetery. He breathed hard, and I felt almost jealous of his eagerness. As things went on, I searched my body, all of the places where I thought I'd tucked away my desperation. All I felt were hands—between my legs, grazing my stomach, buried in the hair at the nape of my neck but never tight enough. He mumbled a sentence into the skin beneath my earlobe, and I refused to parse it. It was too gruff, too consumptive. I felt embarrassed.

I shook him off, and he gladly took my place, lying face-up on the bed. Straddling Jay, I felt evil, struck by a fresh jolt of motivation as I presided over his body. It was always somewhere between faking it and not— the way I would look up at them over my nose, moving lower and lower into their laps; the enjoyment always eclipsed by the need to perform enjoyment, the knowledge I had to enjoy it whether I enjoyed it or not; sliding the button back out through the hole and cringing at my contrived excitement when the fly popped open; always reaching a point of being unsure how much was me and how much was gleaned from some video I'd seen online as far back as the tenth grade that had burned permanently into my mind: *Start slow. Tease. Now, look up. Sad, young, but not too much— that's right. Wet eyes.* Sometimes my mind was so far from the task at hand I'd be a fool to believe it was all my doing, that I had any desire at all for what was taking place. And yet...

He was in my mouth, and he looked helpless. The part where you imagine for a second that you have power, that since you're up there and he's down there it means you're in charge. Maybe it was true, just this one time. The lust-tinged sheen of his eyes kept catching the light. I was seeing what he must have seen just a few minutes before, feeling his feelings. I was so much younger, and he was so much older, but here I was—he had gotten me, somehow. He didn't have to tell me what to do. I was already right there, and my mouth was so warm. Still, though, I was 22— there must still be so little I had done, not just in this context but in general. There was no way I had ever truly been made love to. It was simply never done. The ones I'd been with before were subpar and too naïve to have any real interest in the art of it. He would show me this, someday, when I was ready and sufficiently relaxed and when he had it in him to stop me from doing the things I was doing to him, which I was so fucking good at. My mouth was so warm. He would light candles. He would show me what it could be like. And fuck, I would love it. He would show me so many things. He would. He would.

He was so much older than me, and I was so young. I had so much left to see. I was completely naked now. Both of our clothes were on the floor. I lived here, sure, but only for a few years. It was clear I didn't know the city well. Probably ordered all of my food online, from an app. Drank cheap beer. Everything always bottom-shelf. That's what it was like for him in those days. How much he would have loved someone to show him around, get a good meal in his stomach. A change of pace. He would do that for me, and I would be so much better for it, and my hips were so soft, rolling in the palms of his hands. Some days he would just pick me up after work on a whim and take me out for Thai, or pizza, and he would watch me clean the plate completely and he would ask, *How do you like it?* And I would say, *Ugh, it's so fucking good. I've never had anything like this.* And he'd say, *Yeah?* And I'd say, *Yeah. I never had it like this. It's good it's so good.* And he'd say, *Yeah.* And I'd say, *It's so good it's so good* and feel him shudder inside me, and I'd shudder too.

THE WORLD'S LONGEST KISS

When we woke up the next morning, we decided to go to Waffle House. While it didn't exactly align with my prior fantasy of being Shown The Ropes, I had never actually been to a Waffle House, so there was a loophole. Plus, it was only 9:00 in the morning—not a good hour for curry or pizza. Quickly I realized that Jay was one of those people who wanted to get going immediately upon waking up in the morning. You didn't get that impression from messaging him or from hearing him talk about waking up and going into work, but that tendency was there. It was relieving, in a way, because there was no time or space to feel awkward about having woken up next to him looking twelve times as hungover as I was and only wearing a shirt. Instead, I felt irritated by him immediately. The exasperation took the edge off.

"Can't we at least have a cup of coffee here first?" I negotiated from under the blankets, watching him swipe on deodorant in the room's single beam of dusty yellow light.

"There's no coffee," he said. "Machine hasn't worked for months."

I sighed. At least that explained his eagerness to get out of the house. "How do you live?"

"I dunno. I buy it. It's like a dollar."

I reached down to pick up my pants from the floor and shook my phone out of one of the pockets. It was dead, of course. Nothing to distract me with, nothing to read, just my face staring back at me through the unresponsive black screen. "My hair looks like shit," I said. "I need to shower. I'm gross."

"Help yourself."

"Thanks." I stood up and felt my feet fail to sink through the hard, nubby carpet.

"It's down the hall. The room with the—"

"The blanket," I said. "I know."

"Alright, well, you never know."

"Yeah," I said, laughing for some reason.

Jay stopped fishing around in his drawers and turned around, watching me gather my clothes from the floor. All of a sudden, he said, "You have no idea how much I wanna follow you in there." It was hot and out of place all at the same time, just like the rest of it.

"Yeah?"

"Yeah, but Scott's home, I think."

The roommate. "Ah, right."

"Plus, you probably just wanna get the thing done."

I nodded. "Yeah, I guess I do."

"Alright, well go ahead. Faster you get out, faster we get waffles."

"And coffee."

"And coffee. That's right." We both smiled at each other, and as I turned around to leave, I heard him add, "You sure I can't come?"

I laughed, but I didn't reply. The flattery was nice, but he was right—I did just want to be alone. I made my way down the long hallway to the bathroom, pushed the blanket-door aside, and slipped in. There was a switch beside the one for the light that I assumed turned on an exhaust fan of some kind, but when I flicked it on, nothing happened. And why should I have been surprised at the lack of amenities, considering that the room didn't even have an actual door? It was all just variations on a theme.

The shower was gross in a way that was simultaneously endearing and personally humiliating. This contradiction had been an obvious theme of the past 24 hours. I wondered how many more times and in how many more ways I would encounter this uncomfortable paradox of feeling. The obvious differences between us are constantly complicated by the fact that he still seemed so young in both good and bad ways, leading me to wonder which of my habits would change someday, which wouldn't. If I never grew into a person who regularly cleaned their bathroom, it would look like this in 23 years. A sobering thought.

The water ran. I watched a clump of mold detach from the corner of the shower floor and be swept up by the current toward the drain. I realized I didn't have a towel. I left the shower running and made my way back down the hall to Jay's room. The door was shut now. I knocked gently and for some reason didn't wait for a response before I cracked it open, slowly, quietly. He was lying there on the bed, the lights still down, the morning sun still projecting a single, bright rectangle onto the floor in front of the dresser. When I'd gotten up that morning, he'd still been vaguely dressed, but now he wasn't, his shorts and socks strewn on the floor near the leg of the bed. For a brief second, not knowing what to do, I stood there and watched him. I wondered what he was thinking about, recognized that I probably knew, hoped, and feared that I did.

When he looked over, there was no recoil or desperate humiliation. He let go of himself and curled onto the bed in a less-rigid position—quickly, but not overly so. I wasn't supposed to see this, but he didn't seem bothered. "Hey, what is it?" It was like nothing had happened like this was in no way weird.

"I need towels," I said. I felt like I should make some acknowledgment of what I'd seen, but following his lead meant instead listening to his reply, nodding, and grabbing a towel from the narrow closet I'd somehow missed. I was just cooling down from the unnecessary intimacy I'd just experienced when a voice

I'd never heard before made me whip around, dropping the towels on the floor.

"Morning."

Scott was standing a few feet from me, leaning in the kitchen doorway with a coffee like a guy in a sitcom. He was more normal than I was expecting, wearing a button-down and khakis. I felt a small twinge of embarrassment knowing that a serious middle-aged man had seen me scurrying back and forth from Jay's room. He looked like a guy who was going to put in some Serious Hours at The Office–which prompted the question of why he was so okay with the current state of the apartment's only bathroom.

"Morning," I said back to him, doing one of those flat-lipped nods. I felt him continue to watch me as I continued down the hall and slipped back behind the blanket.

After I finished getting ready, Jay drove us to Waffle House. When we finished eating, we went on this ridiculous road trip, sharing joints and music in the car for hours, taking turns choosing which road or exit to take. He'd lived around here his whole life, so we never got lost. At one point, I nodded off, and when I came to again, we were in the mountains. When I asked where we were, he said it was just two hours from home, just a few counties away, and I said I was surprised you could drive out to somewhere like this in a day.

"I do it all the time," he said, grinning at me in between glances at the road. "I wouldn't be sane without it."

"Well, thank goodness for small favors."

"Ha," he said.

There were a lot of long silences, punctuated by Jay's requests for certain music, which I queued up on my phone, watching a seemingly infinite line of trees scroll past me, not getting bored somehow—the pot and the presence of Jay in the car beside me imbuing every second with cinematic weight. We wound down the mountains into a little town that looked like it hadn't been lived in for years—boarded-up businesses clustered on either side of us; dilapidated, brown-yellow sidewalks; a lot of potholes and not much else.

"Damn," I said.

"West Virginia mining towns," he said, somber, knowing this single sentence was more than enough of an explanation for what surrounded us.

"Damn."

"Wasn't always like this, that's for sure."

"Yeah," I said.

We were on what looked like the main road, but it was empty aside from a single truck a few hundred feet ahead going the opposite way. Reaching an intersection, Jay slowed the car, squinting at the signs and down the road in each direction. "Left, or right?"

"I don't know," I said. "Maybe we should turn around and not go much farther. I don't want you to drive too far back."

He blew a small bit of air out of his nose. "Don't worry, babe. I know where I'm going."

"Alright," I said. "But I don't know."

"Can't go until you pick one."

"I don't know," I said. "Whichever way you want, I guess."

"You're no fun," he joked.

"The light's green. Come on," I said, laughing, some vague annoyance lurking at the edges. "You pick."

"Nobody's behind us; don't worry about it. Just pick one. If we get lost, we get lost." He had that goofy glint in his eye. "Here."

Jay pulled me toward him by the shoulder and kissed me. It was the first time he'd kissed me since the night before, and it took this kiss to make me remember what kissing Jay felt like. I could have sworn before there had been fanfare—now all I could feel was the lack of it. Like kissing a friend. Less than that. Like neutrally placing my mouth against another mouth, completely devoid of context. His tongue felt impossibly large and long inside, and I spent the whole time trying to manifest a feeling of satisfaction, of completion. Then, he separated from me, sensing somehow that the light had turned green. I wiped my mouth with the back of my hand and felt guilty when he looked over.

"I think that might have been the world's longest red light," he said. I agreed, but the look on his face made it clear something got lost in translation.

I looked ahead at the road with a nervous laugh. "Yeah."

Jay's grin widened, and he looked at me expectantly.

"Oh," I said. "Turn right."

Jay needed a break from driving, so we pulled over in some other empty town a half-hour later. There was a park, or really a field, with some trees at the back. Having kicked off my shoes, I curled up with my feet on the dashboard, looking at nothing. Jay stepped out of the car to take a piss in the woods. The street was quiet, swerving a few meters ahead into what was undoubtedly another stretch of rural, mountain emptiness with no shoulder to park on. According to my phone, it was 4:00. If we left now, it would be dark by the time we got home—or at least I assumed. By this point, I had no idea where we were. I could sneak a look at my GPS and see how many miles we were from the city, but that didn't mean anything with Jay at the helm. We'd spent so much time in the car together by this point and hardly any on the highway. I used to like that.

After a few minutes, Jay came around to the driver's side and tapped the window, which I rolled down. "Wanna walk?"

"Yeah," I said. "I guess."

Jay shrugged. "Figured we should stretch our legs. It's nice out."

"Yeah, alright."

I rolled the window up and stepped out of the passenger side. The sun was out, but it was deceiving. I pulled my sleeves down over my arms and the lower hem of my shirt further down my waist, feeling naked in the cold.

"Are you cold?" Jay asked, brushing his hand back through his hair. "I have a jacket in the car."

"No, that's okay."

"You sure? Come on, you're freezing."

"Fine, I guess. If you don't mind."

"Sure, hold on. It's in the trunk."

I leaned against the side of Jay's car as he popped the trunk. He reappeared a minute later with a thick, red flannel that was pilling and perma-creased from months or maybe years in storage.

"No clue how long I had this thing in there," he said, reading my reaction to the site of it. "But hey, we're putting it to use."

"Yeah," I said.

Jay held it up as if to put it on for me, but I pulled it out of his hand and shrugged it on by myself instead. It smelled like mold — like upchucked magic mushrooms — and the tag was itchy.

"Good?" he asked, and I nodded.

As we set off through the tall grass, it occurred to me that this wasn't a park, just a vacant field on the side of the road, maybe even someone's private property that they'd left to the deer, chiggers, and ticks. Jay pointed out an old-looking picnic bench at the far end, about a hundred meters away. He noticed it while taking a leak in the trees and decided that was as good a destination as any, and I agreed. I was okay until the wind hit. Then I huddled even deeper into Jay's big, itchy shirt, keeping my breath shallow to avoid the smell.

"Hot date?" Jay asked eventually, laughing. We'd been mostly quiet, our silence interrupted only by the occasional car whooshing past his parked sedan.

"What?"

"You're going so fast," he said. "What's the rush? You wanna go back?"

"I dunno." I shrugged.

"You feel sick or something?"

"Yeah, a little." It was true. I didn't know exactly when it had started, this dizziness that had been slowly warping everything until it was all too sharp and slightly breathing. I'd been pushing it down, telling myself that it would go away if I did, urging myself that this couldn't happen here in a field in the middle of nowhere with Jay—the worst possible spot.

We slowed down. "Yeah," Jay said, frowning as he looked me over. "You look green."

"Yeah," I said.

"Was it the Waffle House?"

"No. This happens to me," I said. "I'll be fine. I just wanna sit down."

"On the grass? Just wait a minute; we'll get you to the car."

"Okay."

The next few minutes are missing. It was only when I pressed my hand against the cool exterior of the car that I came back into my body. Jay was standing behind me, helping me shirk the thick flannel. "Take this off. You're probably overheated."

I nodded.

"Doesn't make sense. You were shivering before."

"Yeah, as I said, this happens." I was starting to feel more myself with the cool air penetrating the thin fabric of my shirt. Still, Jay and the field behind him had that look to them, that impossible level of detail that made me feel nauseated and lost.

Jay furrowed his brow, a moment of hesitation before walking away from me. The sound of the trunk slamming shut seemed to come in at all angles, and with it, this dome of thick air that in an instant seemed to be suffocating me. My entire body was urging me to hit the ground, so I squatted, soaking the curb and the grass behind with clear, bitter vomit. Startled by the sound of it, Jay had come back around from behind the car to see me retching onto my shoes.

"No more Waffle House for you," he said.

"It wasn't that," I said, still coughing up the last bit. "It's my head."

"Your head?" Jay asked before disappearing again in the trunk of the car.

"Yeah," I said, slowly relaxing from my clenched position. It was rare that things ever got so bad that I vomited, but when it did happen it always made me feel better. I tried to focus on that— the relief of it—and not the fact that Jay had just seen me lose my breakfast all over the road.

Jay came back holding a bottle of water, which he handed to me. "Emergency water," he said.

"Thanks."

"Do you feel better now at least?"

I took a long drink, wincing as the water washed the last residues of barf down my throat and reintroduced it to my taste buds. "Yeah."

"What is it? Like, a migraine?"

"No. My head doesn't hurt."

"Just a stomach thing?"

"I don't know," I repeated. "It just happens. Everything gets overstimulating, and then I start thinking too much about it, and it gets worse."

"And then you throw up."

"Not usually."

"Sounds like panic to me."

"Maybe." Jay handed me the flannel, and I wiped my mouth and nose on the sleeve.

"You should go to a doctor or something," Jay said for no particular reason. I knew he cared about me, but in this instance, it was clear he just needed something to say.

"Nah," I said. "It's been happening forever. Usually, if I go outside or sit down it goes away. And if I don't barf, it's just like, tripping balls I guess."

"What? Like, you get visuals?"

"Kind of, but I meant more like I blackout. Or, I guess, I see myself from far away, kind of."

"What, like, dissociating?"

"Yeah," I said, "I guess. It's seriously not a big deal, usually, I handle it."

"If you're sure." Jay took the flannel back with zero squeamishness, barely avoiding the place where I'd wiped my face as he sloppily folded it and placed it back in the trunk. "You look better at least. You looked like you were on death's door back there."

"Gee, thanks."

He chuckled, and we both stared out at the field for a while. At the back of it was the picnic bench, the destination we'd never actually reached. Maybe if I'd been able to hold it all together for just a few more minutes, maybe if I hadn't walked so fast or if Jay hadn't asked about it, we'd be sitting there now; I'd be calming down, and Jay wouldn't have just watched me croak a full pint of liquified waffles onto my shoes.

"I see there were casualties." Jay pointed down at my feet, as if on cue.

I sighed. "It's fine."

"We'll put them in a bag." He disappeared again around the back of a car and appeared with a plastic shopping bag.

Gesturing to the open trunk, I said, "You keep a lot of stuff in there." I kicked off my shoes and picked them up with the inside-out bag.

Jay shrugged. "I was a boy scout."

The two of us got in the car, and Jay turned the key in the ignition. I kept my head pivoted toward the open window as we pulled away from the curb—away from the field, away from my puke, away from the tiny town in which we'd randomly found ourselves and its world's longest stoplight. I could tell Jay was a little disappointed that our adventure had been cut short, but—

though it seemed wrong to admit it—I felt relieved. At least now he wouldn't try to kiss me.

By the time my head hit the pillow that night, it was 9:00, and I was conflicted. I felt like I'd aged a decade since I'd last been inside my apartment. It always seemed to turn out this way: nothing would happen forever and then a whole thirty percent of my life would come flying straight in my face over a few days. This was, in fact, part of why I felt so conflicted. I was thinking of the way I woke up the morning after Jay and I had been drinking in the park: so reinvigorated to have finally met someone I could get addicted to, someone who was worth getting to know. Before Jay, I couldn't even remember who the last person had been. Certainly not Cody. Certainly not either of the Joes—maybe none of the guys I'd slept with. I'd found chemistry on some rare and unprecedented level, and within weeks of our meeting, something had already fallen flat and it felt weird to touch him, to be far from home, alone. Even the dalmatian seemed disappointed in me, glowering down from its spot on top of the dresser.

He'd even asked if he should come upstairs with me, and I'd turned him down. A perfectly nice person and I'd let things burn out so quickly. It wasn't fair. I told myself that maybe it was just nerves, or my sudden illness, causing this disconnect. My nausea having fully faded, I turned down the lights and conjured a picture of Jay in my mind. I was egging myself on—he's so much older than you, remember the weight of his body, he feels so much—and then, at some point, I must have fallen asleep.

CLASHING PLAIDS

I'd gotten so wrapped up in Jay that when Sidney called me a few days later it was the first time I'd heard from her in a week. I didn't have a great excuse for my long radio silence, seeing as I hadn't told her or anyone else about Jay and I. Luckily, she'd been equally wrapped-up in her newly solidified relationship with Ant. There's this animosity thought to grow between friends when one of them gets a significant other and gradually starts to spend less time with their friends, but I'd never witnessed it. My preoccupation with Jay notwithstanding, I was happy that Sidney was involved in a comfortable, non-whiplash-inducing relationship for the first time since I'd met her. And she'd feel the same about Jay and me, almost certainly, if I were to break the news. Or, at least, I hoped this was still true. We didn't spend much time catching up.

"Are you doing anything today?" she asked almost immediately.

"Nope," I said. I was relieved—it was the first day in a couple of weeks that I hadn't been either working or hanging out with Jay. He'd made some plans with Tom and I'd planned to stay in my pajamas and give my apartment a much-needed deep-clean.

"Cool," she said. "Ant is sick and we were supposed to go to this show tonight."

"Aw."

"Yeah, and I still want to go, so I thought maybe we could go together?"

I hesitated, weighing my general disinterest in these local shows against my desire to catch up with Sidney while we were both available. "Sure."

"I'll pick you up. We can get some food, too."

"Sounds good," I said.

"Cool. I'm thinking, like, six., We can get Thai," she added. "Tom and Jay might meet us there, too."

I froze. "Tom and Jay?"

"Yeah," she said. "Tom mentioned before that they might be going."

Guess those were Jay's mysterious plans.

"Alright," I said, trying to be casual, trying to repress the shakiness in my voice that would surely betray my weird feelings toward Jay and whatever one might call the Thing going on between us. "See you then. Six?"

"Six."

By the time 5:00 rolled around, I was regretting everything. I didn't even like these shows. Wrapped in a towel on the bed, I briefly debated staying there forever, falling asleep, just fucking off. But if there was a non-Jay person I needed to see right now, it was Sidney, and if there was a time to look rushed and tired, it wasn't on a night I expected to run into the twice-my-age guy I'd just slept with and his friend. I located the resolve to find an outfit and dry my hair and made my way outside just as Sidney's car was pulling up.

"Hey," I said.

"Long time, no see," she said, leaning into the passenger side. "You hungry?"

"Yeah."

"Cool." Sidney started the car. "I know we said Thai, but there's this closer place. It's, like, Mediterranean stuff."

"That's fine."

Sidney nodded, pulling a cigarette out of the pack in the center console and placing it on her lips as she felt around for the lighter. After a puff, she said, "So we're having a party."

"We?"

"Ant and me. Like a housewarming thing. To celebrate moving in, I guess."

"Oh, alright, cool." Sensing there was more, I waited for her to continue.

She took another long draw of the cigarette, the light catching on her big teardrop earrings as she turned to ash it out the window. "And Cody's thing." The addition was smooth, matter-of-fact.

My heart dropped. "His thing?"

Sidney sighed. "So, Cody got this job in Toledo."

"Yeah?"

"Yeah, so he's moving."

"Okay, but not, like, soon."

"Kind of soon," she said. "He found a house out there. His friend, I guess—one of the guys from the record store moved out there and he has an extra room."

"Oh."

"It seems good for him."

"I guess," I said.

There was a pause. I let her navigate.

"You know you broke up with him, right?"

"Yeah?"

"I'm just saying..." I didn't know if it was intentional or just the traffic requiring extra focus, but she seemed peeved at me. "It's not like he's leaving town to hurt your feelings."

"I know," I said, hiding my hurt. "It just seems sudden, that's all."

Sidney shrugged, still seeming disengaged. "That's how it happens."

I wanted to ask her what exactly she meant but felt scared of what she knew.

After a short, quiet drive, we parked in a corner garage a few blocks from the restaurant. There were spaces outside, but it made more sense to keep the car in one place and walk back to it after the show. Forsaking the dark garage for the sunlight seemed to improve both of our moods, and we could talk about other things.

"This place is good," said Sidney. "I wanna get pita chips."

"Seems good to me."

"We probably have to eat quick. The place is like—" she looked at her phone, though it was obvious it wasn't displaying anything relevant to our discussion "—a ten-minute walk."

"Alright, cool."

When we reached the entrance, I was starting to feel comfortable again, cleansed of whatever weird energy had transpired between Sidney and me in the car. Even the looming inevitability of running into Jay and Tom seemed bearable, somehow. I would get a drink, have some pita chips, walk over to the venue with Sidney, and things would be fine. My newfound confidence quickly vanished, however, when I saw a familiar silhouette sitting with its back towards me at one of the corner tables.

"Oh shit," Sidney said before I could say anything or even process the encounter. "Hey!"

Tom's chair squeaked against the floor as he rose from his seat and hurried over to us. "Hey," he said, his open-mouthed grin like a golden retriever's.

"Clashing Plaids tonight?"

"Yeah," Sidney said. "That's where we're headed after this."

"Nice. The pregame." Tom nodded, adjusting the opening of his t-shirt sleeve around his bicep.

I hadn't noticed before how muscular Tom was, even though the night we met involved wading naked in a creek together. Maybe I was just overthinking things to keep my eyes and my mind off of Jay, who I now knew without a doubt was the person I'd noticed a moment ago, still seated at the table and facing the opposite direction. As if reading my mind, Tom gestured behind him at the table a few feet away. "I'm over there with Jay if you wanna join us."

Sidney shot me a look whose meaning was unclear, seeing as she didn't wait for my input before responding. "Yeah, sure," she said, and then it was decided: the four of us would sit together.

I took a seat across from Jay, keeping my head down. In my desperation, I'd convinced myself I could avoid the weirdness by seeming busy and just staring at my phone for no reason. But such a strategy would have required some kind of mutual understanding between Jay and me, and as things stood, he had no reason to think things were weird between us.

"Long time no see," he said, the glint in his eye letting me know this was the closest he'd come to acknowledging what had taken place. He slipped his menu to me, and I took it, happy to have another venue for my attention.

I laughed, full of relief. "Yeah."

"Clashing Plaids?"

I looked up. "What?"

"The band?"

"Oh," I said. "Yeah."

Why was this a thing that always happened with these smaller local bands? What was it about them that made people think that saying the name in and of itself was master-level signaling or could pass as decent conversation? It reminded me of a guy I worked with. He had a strategy for easing the weirdness of waiting for the break room's microwave by pointing out what you were eating. He'd just gesture at your cup of soup as it spun in the window and say, "Chicken noodle today," in a neutral tone of voice. What was behind the decision to make things weird for the other person when you could just as easily say nothing?

"You like them?"

"I don't know," I said. "Sidney invited me."

"She doesn't really do local shows," Sidney piped up from behind her menu. "She only comes to these when I drag her."

"Huh, I see," said Jay. "That makes sense."

"It makes sense?" I asked.

"Yeah." Jay turned to me. "I don't know. You strike me as more of a 'quiet night alone,' kind of girl."

"Oh, for sure," added Sidney.

"Yeah, like, she'd much rather have a glass of whiskey and put on a record." He was talking to Sidney but flashed a glance at me, proving the reference was intentional.

"Why are you guys talking about her like she's not here?" Tom swallowed the last of the drink he'd been nursing and gestured over to me with his palm. "It's weird."

"Oh," said Sidney, "we can talk about you if you want."

"Go ahead," he said. "I don't mind being objectified. You know that."

"Shut the fuck up!"

Tom laughed, paying no mind to Sidney's half-assed attempt to shut down his flirting. "I'm just saying, let the woman speak."

"It's fine," I said, reaching no one.

We were all quiet for a second, and I took the opportunity to peruse the menu. We were running out of time for a full meal, but maybe we could all split something light over drinks. Seemed like the best way.

Jay cleared his throat at a volume that seemed to rouse only me.

"Anyway," he said, "I was going to say you'll probably like them. The band. They're no PJ Harvey, but you know."

"Nobody is."

"Amen, babe." Jay held up his drink, a one-sided toast to me.

Whatever weird bantering match Sidney and Tom had gotten into, I felt glad for it—neither of them was paying enough attention to notice Jay's eyes smiling at me over the rim of his drink.

Despite Jay's projections to the contrary, I did not enjoy the music. I spent most of the night standing there, bobbing my head with a kind of impostor syndrome. Needless to say, I was happy when the lights came on and the four of us were spitting back out onto the sidewalk, somewhat stoned, our ears ringing.

"So, that's Clashing Plaids," Jay said.

We were walking side-by-side a few feet behind Sidney and Tom, and I was trying to beam signals through the back of Sidney's head. *What are you doing? Where are we going? What about Ant? Don't you think we should go home? Can you drive right now?*

"What'd you think?"

I shrugged.

"I don't know."

Jay laughed. "Not your thing, I guess." Noticing my focus on Sidney and Tom, he pointed at them and asked. "Sidney your ride?"

"Yeah."

"You're welcome at mine, too, if you want." With the rest of our posse occupied, his hand on the small of my back went completely unnoticed, sending a pulse of conflicting heat through my body.

"I don't know, won't it be weird?"

"Why would it be?"

"What am I going to tell Sidney?"

"I'll tell Tom I'm taking you home, and he'll deal with her."

I sighed. "She has a boyfriend though."

"What?"

"Well, you said he'd 'deal with her.'"

"So?" Jay laughed. "Not everyone is this depraved." He shifted his hand slightly, re-centering me in the simultaneous pleasure and awkwardness of it. "Except us."

"Sidney's a big girl. She drove here, right? She can do what she wants."

"If you don't think it's weird."

"Nah. I'll just tell them you're coming over to pay me back for dinner the other night." He sped up his stride, flashing me a mischievous smile as he looked over his shoulder.

"You wish."

"You're right."

Jay negotiated the separation, and a few minutes later I watched Tom and Sidney disappear into the parking garage where she and I had arrived hours before. All of the unresolved feelings from the other day with Jay quickly crystallized in the pit of my stomach. The moment had come for me to dig deep and count up whatever chemistry was left, to decide exactly how to proceed.

Heading for the car, we were mostly quiet. The street was crowded, demanding our focus to not get separated or bump into other people. At this point, it still wasn't even clear to me what was about to happen—whether we were going back to Jay's place or he was dropping me off at mine. My strategy thus far had been to remain completely passive, to not indicate enthusiasm in either direction. It was weird how Jay didn't seem to have noticed.

"I'm sorry," Jay said eventually as we turned onto the street where he'd parked his car.

"For what?"

"You seem, like, prickly," he said. "I felt like I was being weird, or something. So, I'm sorry."

So, he had noticed. "I don't know. I don't think I'm prickly. I don't really know what I am." It was such a non-answer, but I honestly wasn't lying.

"Well, look, if you just want to go home, that's okay. I'll drop you off."

"I don't know what I want, though."

"I know," Jay said, somewhat insistently. We were standing in front of his car now, but for some reason, neither of us was getting in. "I just don't want you to feel, like, pressured."

"I don't."

"Okay," he said.

I slid into the passenger seat and Jay into the driver seat. The car smelled new inside, and for a second I imagined that none of the events of the past few months had happened, that Jay was just some guy I happened to have met at a show and was letting drive me home. Except that I couldn't imagine a scenario in which this would have taken place. I didn't go to shows like this. I was always so weird and afraid around older people like they were judging me like they were scumbags with weird intentions. There was this cultural divide. And I'd always been way too anxious to just get in a car with someone I hardly knew. In a way, it was miraculous that any of this had even managed to happen at all. Jay had somehow been in the right place at the right time — specifically, Sidney's parents' house the weekend after I broke up with Cody — and the rest was history. What did we even have in common?

"I'm sorry, too, about the puke thing."

"Seriously, it's fine," I said, admittedly with more force than I intended.

"I know. You probably don't want to talk about it." Jay paused for a moment. He still hadn't started the car, and the absence of the ignition sound was as palpable as anything. "I just don't want you to feel weird."

I sighed.

"What?"

"It's just like, you keep telling me you don't want me to feel weird, but you worrying about me feeling weird *makes* me feel weird."

"Okay."

"Okay?"

"I don't get what you mean."

"I know." I looked at Jay's face.

There had been moments before where he'd looked less-than-ecstatic with me, but this was the first time he seemed seriously disappointed. His eyes looked as far away as they did concern, and still, as always, a little too wet in the corners—a reminder that underneath all of the social tiptoeing and the social expectations and the generational gaps was a real person whose feelings for me and about us were serious and real. And I didn't like it.

"Maybe I'm just in a bad mood. I just—" I looked out the window, trying to put together a combination of words that wouldn't completely ruin him, "—don't want to think too much about anything."

Ironic, since I was now the one trying not to make the other person feel weird.

"Then don't," he said. "Just tell me where we're going."

"Okay," I said. "I think I just want to go home."

"Okay." Jay turned the key in the ignition, and off we went.

The silence was so bad, but it seemed worse to put on music. We'd gone this way before, after the night with the brownies and PJ Harvey. The vibe tonight was not much different. Looking at passing cars, looking over the guardrail at the city below, imagining a person much more put-together than me enjoying a relaxing night alone with their thoughts. At some point, there must have been a time when I could spend a weekend in bed reading books or watching movies and not feel this compulsion to make plans, to be with someone. I couldn't remember that being the case, but it had to have happened at some point. Right? What I couldn't understand was when it had changed for me and why.

"Are you doing anything next weekend?" Jay asked out of nowhere.

We were coming off of the highway and getting closer to my building, which probably motivated him to lock down plans with me while we were still face-to-face.

"Um, yeah," I said, feeling instantly sick. "Sidney's party."

"More skinny-dipping?"

I managed a chuckle. "No, it's for her and Ant. She's moving in with him, so it's like a housewarming thing."

"And Ant's the boyfriend?"

"Yeah."

"Mm." The turn signal clicked as Jay focused forward on the windshield, thinking.

"So, what's the problem?"

"It's also, like, a going-away thing for Cody."

"Shit."

"Yeah," I said. "He's moving to Toledo."

Jay snorted. "What's in Toledo?"

"A job and, like, one specific dude apparently that he's going to live with."

"You sound really surprised."

"Well yeah, I am."

"I don't know." Jay was responding slowly, taking extra care in choosing his words. "I say good for him. Go where you're wanted."

"Jesus."

"No, I mean, you did what you needed to do, too. Just, you know." He stayed focused on the road ahead of us, and I struggled to read his eyes. "The fountain."

"Yeah, yeah. I know."

"So, are you going to go?"

"Yeah, I guess. Unless you don't think I should."

"I say do it. It might be the last time you see him."

"Yeah." I left some space, trying to give the impression that the silence was because I was thinking and not because of my feelings. "I'll probably go."

"It won't be fun," Jay said.

On some level, I liked this. We'd regressed slightly to the way things were before they became physical and, therefore, complicated. Sitting in the passenger seat of his car while he gave me advice about Cody and the breakup. I couldn't help but think things may have been better if they stayed this way.

"I know," I said. "Thanks."

A few minutes later we were pulling up in front of my building.

"Hey, listen."

I was about to push the door open when Jay piped up at a louder volume than anything he'd said for the rest of the ride.

"I know you're busy next weekend, but maybe Monday night or something I could come over?"

"You're inviting yourself over?"

"Why not?"

"I mean, it's fine. Just there's really nothing to do here."

"Eh." Jay half-frowned. "We could watch a movie. I would say to come over but I should give Scott a break."

I winced internally, remembering my single, weird encounter with him on my way to the shower.

I hadn't said anything, so Jay continued. "I want to see you."

To my credit, it had been a long few days—everything that had transpired since the Exit Interview had been taxing. Or maybe it went back even farther than that—back to the cemetery, to Taco House, to the breakup. Either way, I still didn't understand exactly why I started crying. Once the tears came, though, they were about everything. The queue had been piling, and now, in the front seat of Jay's car, we would deal with the backlog: Sidney ending up with Ant, finally, the way it felt like some kind of betrayal. Wanting Jay, then having him, then no longer wanting him anymore. Cody, of course—not just the breakup, but the reasons for it, the exhaustion that felt permanent. How you wear down a little more every year you spend trying to know someone, doing what you think is loving them, never convinced that they love you. Those fleeting revelations the relationship you're part of has nothing to do with the other person, that you're the only one in it. It's you behind the curtain, orchestrating every conversation, building the goalposts for your validation, and then picking up his body and throwing him through them. You can realize this over and over again and it doesn't matter. Nothing sticks. Most of the time all you know is that it should be effortless, and it's not, that you should be happy, and you're not. You have no one to blame but yourself for all of the time you've wasted and can't get back. And when you finally end it, that's your fault, too. Seeing his face at the end is the worst part, knowing if you wanted to make him feel something all you had to do was leave, or try to.

And where did that come from, anyway? Where was that depth for the other four years of it, when you were lonely and self-blaming for all of the things he couldn't or wouldn't feel? Somehow being hurt by you is just another way he hurts you, and no one understands it because you're the one who decided to leave. You're supposed to thrive, now, make his pain worth something. You're supposed to shave your head and post a photo of yourself at the top of a mountain like some toxically-positive lifestyle guru. How were there still things to prove now? Prove you had a reason to leave. Prove you still exist without him. Prove that throwing in the towel doesn't make you naïve or stupid. It was all too fucking much.

"Hey," Jay said as I gravitated slowly toward his left shoulder. "Hey, hey, hey, hey, hey. Okay, okay."

He was patting my back and shushing me, the ultimate expression of weird, paternal compassion, but I didn't care. I was already crying, so all I could do now was keep doing it, keep crying. I sat there with my face in his shoulder like that for a good ten minutes, and then when the tears slowed down, I let go and wiped my nose with the back of my hand.

"Are you okay?" Jay asked. It was better when my face was in his shirt and I couldn't see his expression. "You want me to go upstairs with you?"

"No," I said. "That's okay."

"If you're sure."

"Yeah." I sniffed hard and pushed the passenger door open with a weak smile.

"Hey." As I was pulling away, Jay placed his hand on my leg. "Monday. We're watching a movie, okay? We'll talk more about it. Okay?"

"Okay," I said.

NO WILDERNESS

I almost didn't recognize Jay when he showed up at my building on Monday night. He'd called to let me know that he was downstairs, but when the elevator opened, the only thing I saw was a stocky guy with a shaved head standing outside the main doors. Fortunately for me, he thought my initially ignoring him was some kind of joke and played along until I recognized him.

"You shaved your head!" I was trying to sound pleasantly surprised rather than horrified.

"Yeah." He ran his hand over his freshly-buzzed scalp. "I do this every few months, just about. It's a good refresh."

"Oh," I said. "Makes sense."

We were in the elevator, and I still couldn't get over it. It wasn't that he looked bad—he didn't—it was that he looked like a completely different person. The shaved head made him look older, somehow the lack of a beard enhanced the effect, and the result was a face I could no longer divorce from the generation that had also produced my parents. Somehow, I'd managed to avoid this line of thinking before, but now it was over: I was standing in an elevator with someone old enough to be my father.

Our first moments in my apartment did nothing to assuage my discomfort. "Oh," Jay said, gesturing at the faux-wood particle-board furniture bookshelf and chairs. "Everything matches."

"Yeah." I swung my keys around my finger, letting them slide off onto the kitchen counter. "It all came furnished."

Jay kicked his shoes off and lined them up against the baseboard by the door before sitting down in one of the two kitchen chairs. He looked stupidly tiny crouched over the table like he was on the set of some cheaply-staged play.

"So, that thing Tom said about how all of our apartments look the same?" I reached into the freezer and pulled out a bottle of Canadian Club I'd been keeping.

Jay laughed. "Yeah, I mean, your place looks just about exactly as I expected it to look."

"And that is?"

"I don't know," he said. "It doesn't really look like you. It just looks like a place you rent in your 20's and then leave."

"Sorry," I said, reaching up into the cupboard and pinching the rims of two glasses in my thumb and fingers. "You want me to hang up a blanket in front of the bathroom so you feel more at home?"

"Alright, alright."

I placed the glasses and the whiskey on the table in front of Jay. "Big pour or little pour?"

"Come on," he said. "Big pour."

As we drank our whiskey, I watched Jay's eyes scan around the room—the top of the fridge, the sink piled with dishes, the empty wall beside the door where he'd carefully arranged his shoes.

"Are you looking for something?" I asked eventually.

"Yeah, where's that dalmatian?"

I grinned into my cup, pleasantly surprised at his show of curiosity as opposed to judgment. "Guard Dog's in the bedroom."

"Ah." Jay finished the last of his whiskey and set the glass down on the table. "So that's how you lure them in."

"Who's 'them?'" I asked with a sort of playful exasperation. "The only person who cares about this dog is you."

"What about Cody?" he teased.

"Yeah, but that was..."

"Come here."

There it was again, that same tone from the car on the day I threw up. Mechanically, without giving much thought at all to what I wanted, I was coming toward him, being pulled there. He scooched the chair back and accepted me with a kiss and a quiet grunt onto his lap. The whiskey-tinged cold mint on his breath tasted antiseptic, and his freshly-shaven face only furthered the clinical feeling. He was, even down the physicality, a stranger. It only took me a few seconds to pull away.

"You okay?"

"Yeah."

"Good," Jay said, grinning.

I let him continue to kiss me. I don't know why I let this go on. I was waiting, I suppose, for some definitive feeling of discomfort, of not actively wanting him to touch me. But the most I could manage was a lack of enthusiasm. I barely moved except to follow his lead—stepping forward, opening into the kiss, letting him lead us slowly into the bedroom. A series of tacit agreements that culminated in me lying naked in the center of my bed as Jay crouched between my shins with lidded eyes.

"You're beautiful."

I didn't respond.

His hands were cold, cupping my breast, running their way down my stomach. I couldn't look at him. He shifted in the bed, his body unwieldy and backlit by the light in the other room as he bent to kiss his way up one of my legs. I remained perfectly still, hyper-focused on his shaved head burying itself between my thighs. It was a few more seconds before he paused the action to look up at me and ask again, "Are you okay?"

"Mm-hmm."

"Should I keep going?"

I paused for a second, thinking. "I don't know."

"We can stop."

"Okay," I said.

I looked up at the ceiling, feeling Jay's weight shift around on the bed as he moved next to me. I folded my legs up close to my chest and slipped under the blanket before reaching beside me for the clothes I'd left on the floor.

"Sorry," he said.

"No, it's okay. I'm sorry."

"I just thought you would have—"

"No, I know, it's okay."

"I don't want you to think I'm taking advantage of you."

"I don't." It was weird for him to say this, given I felt the same way.

"You're a genuine friend to me, and I care about you. I just don't want you to think I'm like..."

"I don't." We weren't looking at each other. I pulled my shirt over my head and shoved the rest of my clothes under the sheets, where I pulled them back on out of view.

"I can see myself falling in love with you eventually."

The instant it came out of his mouth, I was upset at him for saying it. It was such an odd, sudden thing to lay out there, especially now. It had only been two nights ago that I'd cried into Jay's shoulder in the passenger seat of his car over a relationship that, despite my actions to the contrary, I had not gotten over.

"That's stupid," I said, my eyes locked far away on the kitchen chair visible through the open door.

"I mean it."

"Stop," I said. "I'm 22 years old."

"So? You already know I don't care about that."

"Doesn't matter," I said. "Like, no offense, but I know you're never going to come with me to meet my parents." Admittedly, I shared this sentiment—I couldn't bear the thought of introducing my dad to a guy who was just two years younger than him.

"Whoa." My eyes were still focused elsewhere, but I could feel Jay's weight shift as he twisted toward me on the bed. "Who said anything about meeting your parents?"

"No, I'm just saying you don't know what you're saying."

"Well, you know what I think," said Jay. "I've said before there are a lot of ways to do—" he gestured vaguely in front of us. "—this."

"Mm." I looked up at the Guard Dog as Jay spoke.

"Just like I don't have to do the whole other thing. Kids, office job, house, whatever. We can do whatever we want with this."

"Yeah, but there's a limit, right? You can't actually go off the grid."

"Who said anything about going off the grid?"

"You know what I mean," I said. "I'm saying at some point we'd have to still be Something, and you'd probably have to meet my parents, and I know you wouldn't want to do that."

"Well, let's imagine for a second. Maybe we stay friends, we keep doing this, maybe we fall in love eventually. And we just have fun. How is that 'off the grid'?"

"We have fun," I repeated.

"Watch movies, go for drives, whatever. We don't have to get married." He said the word married like it was a disease he had just contracted by speaking to me.

"But what if I want to?"

"Why?"

"I don't know!"

"Why can't you be imaginative? There's more than one way to do things."

I sighed. "I know that. But not everything has to be like that. Some things can just be normal. Some things have to be."

"I don't agree with that," Jay said. "I don't think anything has to be. They say that about making enough money to survive in this country, but I'm doing it my way. I don't think anything has to be normal."

"You only feel like that because you're the age you are," I said, knowing I was now treading on the sacred, difficult ground—that I had brought up the one untouchable thing. "You can't do that now."

"Why not?"

"You think I can just, like, find somebody who knows somebody and then end up with a job and a rent-controlled apartment under the table? That's not possible for us."

"Who's 'us'?"

"Like, people my age." I was sitting up in bed now, aimlessly staring around the room to avoid Jay's eyes. "My generation," I added in a purposely stupid voice.

"I'm sure it's harder," he said, "but it's not impossible."

"It might be," I said. "Everything's already used up. There's no wilderness."

"Explain."

"Like, back in the day there was still open space so you could come up with your way of doing things. But now there's a name and a label and a system in place for everything. There's no wilderness."

"So, what? Do you think we didn't have to look for wilderness? It's not easy to forge your path; that's the point."

"I thought the point was to be happy."

"It is," he said. "I just mean if it was easy then everyone would do it."

"Everyone is doing it, now. That's what I mean by no wilderness. Like, when you were 22 and you wanted to do odd jobs for people, you could just ask around. Now there are, like, 37 apps for finding people to do random gig work for you, and then you have to work with them, and they send you 1099s. And there's nobody you know who knows someone because you hardly know anyone, and everything else you do is through an app, too. I'm saying that way of doing things is gone."

"But nobody is saying you have to do things that way."

"No, but I'm saying that's what I mean by everything being co-opted."

"What does this have to do with getting married? Or your parents?"

"Nothing! I'm just saying." I'd been swaying back and forth on the mattress, fidgeting with a hair tie on my wrist. "There's no 'other way of doing things.' I hope you understand."

"I'm sorry, but I don't think I see it that way."

"I know you don't, but it's true."

"I just think you need to be more imaginative."

"Why, because I don't believe you're falling in love with me after having sex one time?"

"We had sex two times."

"What are you talking about? No."

"The PJ Harvey night?"

"We didn't have sex that night," I said.

"We didn't have intercourse," Jay said, blowing through my instant cringe reaction at his use of the world. "We *definitely* had sex."

"I don't agree with that."

"Well, I don't know what to tell you."

"It's fine. Let's just not talk about it."

"Okay." There was a pause, leaving the room silent apart from the sound of the elevator moving up the wall behind the bed. "Do you still want to watch that movie?"

"Sure."

The movie was one neither of us had seen before, but that seemed interesting by the title. It was about this girl growing up in some kind of Mormon community who is convinced she's gotten pregnant with the son of God from listening to a rock song on a blue cassette tape, and that the guy who sang on the tape is the baby's father. After her entire family laughs her off the stage, she steals one of the cars on the Mormon compound and drives into Las Vegas where she meets a bunch of burnt-out, metalhead guys who let her tag along with them. At the end of the movie, one of the guys she was with the whole time decides to marry her and become the father of the baby, and she finds out that the guy who sang on the blue cassette tape was her biological father. Jay kept laughing at everything, and it made me feel stupid for thinking that the movie was beautiful.

When it was over, I had all of these thoughts about how the main character was like Dorothy, and the entire thing was like a warped, modern-day version of *The Wizard of Oz*, but all Jay said was, "That was pretty stupid."

We tried to talk, but it wasn't long before things fizzled out and Jay got up to leave. I put the glasses in the sink, and he offered to wash them. When I declined, he continued over to the door, slipped back into his shoes. "I'll pick the next one," he said before leaving, and I laughed, although I think we both knew this was the last time we would ever see each other.

THE PARTY

It had been at least four or five months since I'd been to a real party—that is unless you counted Taco House, which I didn't. Not really. I hadn't been around this many people my own age in just as long. These were not the ideal circumstances for saying goodbye to my ex for the last time, but I couldn't even remember the last time there were circumstances I could describe as Ideal. Inexplicably, though, it felt like I was the one who was leaving, or maybe that I'd gone away for a long time and just returned. Fiending for the first drink, I paced through each room of Sidney and Ant's house, each one holding a handful of people I could have sworn I'd met before but couldn't remember.

The first person I truly recognized wasn't Ant or Sidney or even Cody, but Tom, who materialized in the kitchen doorway seemingly out of nowhere. It seemed weird that Sidney would have invited him, given their weird entanglement just a month prior. Then again, I'd barely talked to her for the past few weeks. I probably lacked context. I was debating whether it made sense to go up and say hi, in light of Jay and our falling-out, when he waved and began pushing his way through the crowd between us.

"Hey," he said, holding up his cup so it sloshed some unidentified liquid into the kitchen floor.

"Hey!" I yelled over the noise. "I didn't know you were coming."

"Yeah," he said. "Gotta come out and support."

I nodded, despite not knowing what he meant. "Is Jay here?"

We both narrowed our eyes at each other, trying, I assume, to figure out how much the other person knew about what had happened.

"No, just me."

He finished the last of his drink and topped off the cup from a flask he pulled from his pocket. At this point, I was unsure whether age was just a number, but it seemed to be Tom's life's work to prove the axiom true.

"I brought my friend, but I haven't seen her in a bit. I don't know what happened to her."

"Shit."

"Yeah, you'd like her. When I run into her, I'll let you know."

He gave me a weird pat on the shoulder as he passed by to search the rest of the house.

Sidney and Ant were down in the basement, sharing one of those fold-up camping chairs in the corner while a handful of people playing beer pong on a plastic table.

"Happy housewarming," I said, raising my cup at them as I made my way over.

"Thanks," said Ant.

Sidney had been talking for a while now about Ant's newfound commitment to her, but something about seeing her sitting on his lap and smiling at him made it sink in. I felt like I was staring at an old photo of somebody's parents, two people who got married one day and stayed together and would get caught making out by their grown children.

"You guys look happy," I said.

"Thanks," they said at the same time, and then grinned at each other.

I smiled to myself and looked into my cup.

"You know," Sidney teased, crossing one leg over the other as she assumed a regal position on Ant's lap, "when one attends a housewarming party it's customary to bring a gift."

"Ah," I said. "Well, when one invites her best friend to a housewarming party where she doesn't know anyone it's customary to meet her at the door."

Sidney scoffed. "You do know people! You know Cody!"

I raised my eyebrows at her.

"You know Tom!"

"Yeah," I said. "I did see him upstairs. He was looking for some girl or something."

"What? She's right here." Sidney gestured over to the person who had been sitting in the other camping chair beside them, who, until now, I'd been largely ignoring.

"Oh," I said. "Hi. I'm a friend of Tom and Jay."

"Hi," she said, not looking up from her phone, "I'm Anna."

"Wait," I said. "Tarot card Anna?"

She laughed. "Never heard anyone say it that way."

"Sorry. I mean, Jay mentioned you. You make, like..."

"Tarot videos, yeah." A dozen or so plastic bangles swung on her arms as she set her phone down in one cupholder and retrieved her cup from the other. "I'm trying to branch out though."

Ant and Sidney, who had seceded from the larger conversation and formed their nation of two, ended their whispered conversation and got up from their chair, leaving it open for me.

"That's cool," I said, sitting down. "It's weird. You're younger than I thought you would be."

"Why did you think I'd be older?"

"I don't know. You're friends with Tom and Jay, so I figured."

"So are you," she said, shrugging.

I sat awhile, watching the game of beer pong unfold. It was the typical distribution of teams: two guys who appeared to be friends versus a third friend and the girl he was trying to pick up, and the guy kept attempting stupid trick shots to impress her but never landing them. The girl he was with kept laughing at him while also trying to seem worse at the game than he was, while also trying not to seem too ditzy. It was the usual thing, but I hadn't been anywhere like this in a long time, and putting myself in the girl's shoes made me feel exhausted. I thought to myself that I must have been able to do this before, at some point. Not necessarily the beer pong thing but the social tightrope, manning the switches for everybody else's moods and motives. It didn't seem possible now, but at some point, I must have been able to keep all of those things in my head at once.

"Jay told me about the fountain," I said out of nowhere, fearing she would leave before a more organic chance came up.

"The fountain?" Anna was on her phone again, probably responding to YouTube comments or texting one of her friends about this weird person sitting by her at a party.

"Yeah. He said it was this philosophy that you had. Like, about always staying at the fountain, or whatever. Kind of the idea of Six Flags?"

"Oh," she said without looking up. "Yeah. I don't know if it's a philosophy." She dragged the word out, not necessarily slurring but not intentional, either.

"Maybe that's the wrong word," I said. "But you believe in that?"

Anna shrugged, a chunk of dark hair falling into her face as she squinted at her screen. "I mean, yeah, I guess."

"I think it's a cool idea," I said. "Like, a way of saying you should do your own thing and not let anybody take you away from that. Like, stay where you're wanted and don't go after things. Just do things. You know?"

She laughed a little, looking up from her phone at me with this kind of patronizing concern. "Yeah, sure." She finished what looked like the last of her drink, then winced. "Honestly, I didn't really think about it much."

"Oh?"

"Yeah, even the readings I do, it's like—" Anna picked her phone up mid-sentence, squinted at something, and returned it to its place in the cupholder on her right "—I'm not the one doing it. You know?"

"What, like, the ideas just come to you?"

"No," Anna laughed. "Like, whatever I say, it's the other person who makes it into a thing, you know?" She bobbed her head forward at me as she spoke. "Or, what did you say? 'A philosophy,'" she added, in a tone that made it unclear whether she was mocking me.

"Yeah, but I mean, it's a real thing. It might not be called The Fountain, but it's still true."

"I don't know," Anna said. "Is it?"

I blinked at her.

"I need another drink,"

"You said Tom was upstairs, right?"

"Yeah."

"Alright, cool."

She walked past me up the basement stairs, and that was the last I saw of her that night.

With Anna hiding from me upstairs, and Sidney and Ant absent, I wandered the house, looking for a familiar face or, failing that, somewhere reasonable to stand. I should have known not to do this since it's always doing this that you run into the one person at the party that you don't want to see. And there he was, sitting on the bottom stair in the living room, nursing a beer. He waved me over.

"Hey."

"Hey." I peered at the bottom of my plastic cup, wishing I'd re-upped my drink.

"It's so weird about Ant and Sidney," Cody said.

I felt my demeanor brighten a bit. "Yeah." I wasn't sure where things were with Cody, but he was talking to me about something other than the two of us, something I appreciated.

"It's good, though."

"Yeah." I looked over my shoulder, half-expecting Sidney or Ant or even Tom to wander over and rescue me from the encounter taking place.

"I guess you heard I'm moving," he said.

"Yeah."

"Yeah. Toledo." Cody smirked into the lip of his bottle, then sipped it. "Not where I thought I'd end up, but..."

"Neither is this." I made a misleading gesture that implied I was referring solely to this party and not its broader context or the fact that he and I hadn't spoken in weeks.

"True."

A flash.

Cody scooted to one side, letting a guy walk past him up the stairs. Once he'd gone through, I took the space.

"Your mom must be sad," I said.

He shrugged. "Yeah, kind of. It's not that far though."

"Isn't it?"

"No." Cody shook his head. "Like, four hours. I think on a bus it's, like, five and a half."

"Oh," I said.

"Yeah."

"But the job is good?"

"Yeah."

"Good. I'm glad you're, like, doing good."

I could feel him suppressing a laugh as I stumbled over my words.

"Me too."

I took a deep breath. "I'm sorry everything ended up shitty before."

"Nah," he said. "If things had to end up that way, then it's whatever. Now I got this job, and the house is cool, so I'm good."

I smiled, knowing all the while I was hearing the abridged version of events, the version people give family members at holiday dinners rather than the one that's truer but uncertainly fraught. It would have hurt more if it wasn't the way things had always been with Cody and me, even together.

"And hey," he added, "Sidney says you've been busy and stuff, too, so it's good."

Busy. I tried to picture what she might have meant but kept returning—against my will—to the image of my puke being expelled from my body onto the curb in West Virginia.

"Yeah, I guess." He was wrong, but we both deserved diplomacy.

As we sat on the stairs with our drinks, I kept a lookout, terrified someone we knew would see us sitting together and make it all mean too much too fast. But the only people around us were ones I either didn't remember or had never actually met, thinking nothing of Cody or I besides that we were blocking the stairs.

After a few minutes of us looking around at the party and our phones, Cody turned to me.

"Look, sorry if I'm weird, but if you ever want to visit, you're always welcome."

My breath caught in my chest in a way I hadn't anticipated. But, I'll admit, I didn't hate it.

"I'll have to think about it," I said.

He nodded slowly. "I know."

"Thanks."

TOLEDO

I was on the bus, but I didn't know why. I didn't know shit about Toledo, only that he was there and no one was back at home. Sidney and Ant were always busy. I hadn't heard from Jay in a while. It'd been weeks of sitting around on the weekends, and I'd begun to feel like I didn't even exist. So, it was against my better judgment, maybe, when I texted him to tell him I was coming. That conversation at the party felt like it had happened years ago. My memory may have been incorrect—he may not have smiled at me; he may have just been acting polite. Even packing my bags for the weekend, I felt convinced I was fucking up, that this chain of events had been one shitty, extended mistake.

I hadn't slept much the night before and felt like dying. After spending the first hour or so of the ride trying to nap, I'd given up. Each time I fell asleep, a bump in the road would bounce me awake, making me feel worse and the ride longer. The sleep deprivation made it hard to get a handle on my thoughts. I vacillated endlessly between excitement and dread, reminding myself I was coming to visit someone I was comfortable with and knew well, and then reminding myself that we'd recently broken up.

I pulled out my phone to send my umpteenth needy text that day: *you're picking me up at 5 right?*

Three dots appeared on my screen almost instantly.

Yeah.

you don't mind right?

No. I invited you

I kn

I sighed, locking my phone and placing it on my lap. I was on thin ice, physically. I couldn't read this much in a moving bus and shouldn't have been trying. I clenched my body to dispel the static that had been building in the back of my head, shrugging my jacket off to get air on my skin. It was just too hot. Once I cooled down, I would feel less sick, and then maybe I would fall asleep. I just had to cool off.

My phone buzzed against my thigh. I flipped it back over, tempted. It was Cody again.

YOU don't mind right?

I backspaced the partial reply from a few minutes earlier.

no!

see? It's all good.

I flipped the phone back over, clenched harder. I had just made a mistake. The static had returned—and with intensity. I kicked my boots off and twisted to rest my socked feet on the seat beside me, desperate for relaxation and space and air. I was quickly approaching the state I'd reached with Jay in the field, only it was worse in that I was moving and alone. As I leaned back, the heat and nausea and static overtook me, and then the thoughts did. I didn't want to be here. I was making a mistake and things would end badly for both of us, all because I could never just sit with anything, could never just handle being alone, could never exist without the context provided by another person. I should have stayed home.

The girl took a few deep breaths and gripped the headrests on either side of her. She reached behind her and pushed up the back of her shirt, pressing her bare skin to the window. It was cold. It helped. She wasn't that far away now. She just had to hold out for a few more minutes—an hour tops—and then things would feel okay again, and she would be safe with someone, and she wouldn't have to make any decisions.

The girl got off the bus in Toledo. Cody was waiting there, waving. He smiled up at her as she thanked the bus driver and then held her backpack on the way to the car. After dinner, it was only a matter of time before the talk of where she would be sleeping and why came up. And both Cody and the girl pretended to deliberate, even though they knew where she'd end up. And they ended up there. And he touched her.

The girl woke up in his bed every night for the next few days. At the end of the weekend, she realized she would have to go back home, but she didn't want to. She couldn't. She wanted to keep waking up in a warm bed for the rest of her life. So, she stayed in Toledo. She had her things shipped out of her apartment and moved them into the house. And then, every morning, she woke up in a warm bed in Toledo, exactly the way she wanted.

In the mornings, Cody would leave for his job while the girl stayed behind—cleaning the house, keeping it together, watching TV on the couch in the living room, greeting the roommate whenever they passed in the kitchen. When Cody got home, and only then, she would shower. He would stand in the corner, watching her move around under the water, and she would let him. If he felt up to it that day, he'd hold her down in the bed and make her say 'I love your fat cock, you have such a fat cock,' and she would never think twice about it, just say it.

Saturdays, they'd make love, clean, shop for new things for the house. Every single weekend, something new for the house, until they had to ditch the roommate and get a new house entirely, then a bigger one, then a bigger one, and fill it with a son and two massive dalmatians.

It was a nice life. She was happy. From that first night, she wanted for nothing. Cody got a raise and built a swimming pool in the backyard. The next year, a fountain in the front. Some days, when nobody was home, she'd hike up the legs of her pants and wade in, in plain view of the street. The neighbors knew—it was endearing. They'd go up to their windows and watch. If the weather was good, she'd spend hours there, circling, grinning down at the tops of her feet through the perfect water.

Acknowledgments

Writing a novel is a lot of lonely work, and yet somehow putting it all together takes about three entire villages. The non-exhaustive list:

Thank you to Amber Khan for the initial inspiration behind the philosophical concept of *The Fountain*, which I then butchered into oblivion.

Thank you to every bleeding heart online I've had the pleasure of talking shop with. We are the real cool kids' table.

Thank you to *Neutral Spaces* and Giacomo Pope for hosting early chapters of this novel on the *Neutral Spaces* blog.

Thank you to PJ Harvey, Kevin Morby, Van Morrison, and everybody that's ever played me a record.

Thanks, Tiny Rick, Saint Peter, and Saint Paul.

Thanks, Josh, Chanel, and Thirty West for making this all possible.

And thank you B for supporting me, putting up with me, loving me, and listening to me answer my own questions while I pace around the room. I love you so much.

About the Author

Kat Giordano is a poet (1%) and a massive millennial crybaby (99%) from Pennsylvania.

She co-edits *Philosophical Idiot* and works for a law firm, somehow. Her debut full-length poetry collection, *The Poet Confronts Bukowski's Ghost* was published by *Philosophical Idiot* in 2018. She is also the author of many highly embarrassing social media meltdowns.

Look deep into my eyes. Take a deep, cleansing breath and clear your mind. You are getting very sleepy. Kat Giordano is very cool. You like her.

www.ingramcontent.com/pod-product-compliance
Lightning Source LLC
Chambersburg PA
CBHW071105100726
47908CB00008B/2266